You Turn My Pain Into Love

John Tarpley

authorHOUSE®

AuthorHouse™
1663 Liberty Drive
Bloomington, IN 47403
www.authorhouse.com
Phone: 833-262-8899

Published by AuthorHouse 08/06/2021

ISBN: 978-1-6655-3440-6 (sc)
ISBN: 978-1-6655-3446-8 (e)

Library of Congress Control Number: 2021916194

Print information available on the last page.

Any people depicted in stock imagery provided by Getty Images are models, and such images are being used for illustrative purposes only. Certain stock imagery © Getty Images.

This book is printed on acid-free paper.

Chapter 1

Most people said I would not make it to see twenty- two, but I fooled them, and I am here right now today to tell how I survived the ghetto. When I was in my mother's (Mary) womb she was a drug addict, because of that I suffer from seizures while I was in her womb I have forgotten the days of my beautiful Black Nubian African America Queen I would not be in this would most of all the almighty god! Like the scripture says choose light over darkness, my choice is light over darkness my father (Peter) left my mother when she was pregnant with me when she went in to labor and I came into this world my mother held me in her hand and that was the last time I saw my mother and she saw me. I was raised up by all kinds of people who I did not even know, no one would not tell me who my mother was I was staying with a woman and took care of me like a mother would. I stayed with Susan she talked with me and told me who my parents are, my father was in prison, Susan, told me that she was not my mother and I cried, but I was older when she told me this, but when I was five years old Susan gave me back to my aunt Linda because my aunt Linda the one who gave me to Susan to raise because she had her own kids to raise and her husband didn't want me there and I was a baby when Susan gave me back to my aunt Linda, my aunt kept me for a while then gave me to my aunt Gloria, my aunt Gloria abused me, she use to beat me naked in the tub with water all over me, she used to hang from the ceiling fan and beat me; and she used to make me eat soap, sometimes she use to not feed me, she use to make me stand up at night in my room until morning time, she use to take my hand and put it in her mouth and bite my hands, I use to have blisters on my fingers. She used to beat me with sticks and extension cords, she used to slap me down, curse me out, scream at me for nothing, she also uses to push my head down in the toilet while shit was in there. She had a son named Paul and he used to see the things that happen to me, but he could not do nothing but look at what his mother (Gloria) was doing to me I was going to school, and I use to cry at night and ask god why do my aunt do me this way and treat me nasty? My aunt (Gloria) was the one who gave me to Susan. Susan told me that my aunt Linda brought me to her when I was a baby with cigarette burns all over me, and I was sick with blood and cold running out of my nose, my pamper was nasty and I looked like I had not eaten anything for days. I often thought to myself if my aunt Linda loved me so much why did she give me to a lady that was not my family? (v2 Chaka Khan-through the fire) my grandmother (Sarah) uses to watch my aunt Gloria beat me, and my grandmother Sarah use to tell her to stop but she uses to keep beating until she uses to get tired of it. When my father (Peter) got out of prison my aunt Gloria gave me to him, my father got me I was seven years old he talked to me about how he changed his life, I stayed with him, I felt like he owed me and the children that he head on the streets when I was a child my father and I lived in a one bedroom apartment together, he got his wife Vivica back and his son Mark and his daughter Sonya I did not stay with my father very long, so I told my father that I wanted to go home to my mother, so my father took me home to my mother (Mary) I was twelve years old. When my father drops me off to my mother's house I got out of the car, my father said there is your mother I jumped out the car and ran to my mother and jumped up and hugged her and squeezed her neck with tears running down my face. My mother told me to take all my clothes and things upstairs where my sisters and brothers were, after I took all my things upstairs I told my father (Peter) good bye I was scared to be in the house with people I never seen before in my life, my three sisters hug me Keisha, Angie, and Shawn (v3 Toni Braxton; breathe again) I was scared because I never seen them before I also met my two brother's Morris, and Charles they hug me to, when I sat down in the living room I saw how dirty the house was my mother lived in the ghetto I was just happy to see my family. Days went by then I start calling my father and told him to come pick me up because I start seeing my mother and uncles do drugs my mother took care of six children. My uncles (Travis, Howard, Tony, Michael, Lorenzo) live with us and my grandma (Ethel) I had five uncles and we stayed under the same roof; my father would bring me money every once in a while when I ask him to and school clothes. My mother use to leave and go out in the streets for about two or three days before she come back home to us, sometimes she would leave all the time, she would drink with my uncles all the time they would be drunk, they would fight and would argue mostly every day, they would break up almost everything in the house! my sisters and my brother's and I would go days without food, the refrigerator use to be empty most of the time. Most of my life I have been suffering I got tired of living the way I was living finally my mother start looking for jobs even though she was on drugs and drinking alcohol she was on ware fare I drop out of school and started stealing and selling drugs and doing what I had to do to survive and take care of my family, my two brothers Morris and Charles did the same thing, the money my mother was receiving from the government was not enough to support us we were to young nobody would hire us for jobs. I could not go to school or college and take care of my family at the same time. Same people think you can get a job while a mother

3

is struggling hard to care for her children on ware fare. My mother use to cry every day and every night because she did not have the money to take care of us and no man or a father to watch us and she did not want us out stealing, robbing, and selling drugs. I kept going to juvenile and jail. Author, I think that David had all the answers in Deuteronomy 28 it speaks of the curses our people will go through but a mother is supposed to hold on to her children, like Moses mother held on to him although she gave him away Moses kept communicating with his family his sister; and mother reason to believe gain power in thy youth for you never know when it will be your turn to die (v5 Vivian Green). My mother tried her best but never succeeded then my mother was killed in a drive by shooting, I was in jail at that time I talked with my mother that night on the phone in jail, she said to me, I'm tired of stressing, crying, and worrying, your uncles are driving me crazy, god is going to take my life soon I can feel it mother loves you when I'm dead and gone make sure David, Morris, and Charles take care of your sisters, you all just take care of each other forget about your uncles and grandmother. David I love you all, but I am going to die soon, real soon because I am going through too much pain. The next day I woke up in jail I thank god before I got up out of my bed by letting me live to see another day. Later on that day I had a visitation, my mother was supposed to come and see me, but my girlfriend (Cynthia) told me my mother (Mary) was killed in a drive by, I thought she was joking, but she started crying she told me to watch the news when I go back to my cell and I will see it on there, I looked at my sister that was sitting next to her and she said it's true David. My mom was killed, I was shocked, upset, angry, and mad, I was so angry that I tried to break the glass I was looking through, the officers came running to where I was at and grab me and through me on the ground and drag me in to confinement, my sister (Angie) and girlfriend (Cynthia) had left already, they was telling the officers that my mother was killed but the officers did not care they just drag me to confinement because I was yelling, and screaming I was about to go crazy before the officers through me in to the cell they made me take off all my clothes, I was naked. I didn't want to eat anything, all I was thinking about was my mother, crying all day, talking to myself (v6 Heather Headly; in my mind) about to go crazy because something I had so beautiful it was gone all I can think about in that cell was what my mom used to do and tell me that night I talk to her she told me she was going to die she was feeling it, god was going to take her from this world real soon. (v7 Toni Braxton; hands tied) She also told me told me god works in mysterious ways, and most of the time he could be telling you something, you just need to listen, I don't know about you but I listen to god when he talks to me just like my mom use to always say; all them days that past by I was thinking about when my mother past away when I was locked up in that cell naked freezing to death, I was so cold my skin turned white from the cold. Just sitting there thinking about all the times my mom told me to stay out of trouble and do what's right, go to school I did not listen, but now I wish she was living to see that I have changed my life and that I am not living in the ghetto anymore and I'm married David thought about so many things that his mother said to him, referring to how she stands in front of him talking about what's right and wrong. Right now, David would let his mother beat me for to get right in his place. You only have one mother and David had one, but he lost her Mary soul is always with David! Officers use to come in the cell to talk to David he did not listen to them because all he wanted was his mother back, he lost lots of weight a couple of weeks later he went to court

And the judge let him go that day David called his father to come pick him up when his father came and pick him up he was talking with his father while he was driving him home, David ask him to go to his mother's funeral he said no I can't go I beg my father to go to the funeral but he said he already saw her at the awake, but I believe he was lying I felt in my heart that he was lying for that reason, I felt like the reason he didn't want to go was for his wife Vivica well she did not get along with my mother (Mary) I really wanted him to go but it broke my heart that he didn't care for my mother I forgave him because if I did not forgive how can I ask god for forgiveness. I still think about my mother how beautiful she was, we had our good days and bad days, but we still stuck together just like it is said in the book blood is thicker than water when my father dropped me off I slammed his door and told him thank you! When I turned around I saw that everybody was getting ready to go to my mother's funeral god does work in mysterious ways and trying to tell you something because that day I got out of jail (v9 Whitney Houston; step by step) and came home was the day of my mother's funeral all my family members were ready to go, David said he was filthy and dirty because he's been in jail all that time, so David left with his family and went to his mother's funeral just as he was cause it was too late for him to clean his self-up and dress up. I didn't care I was just thankful to be there and to go to this funeral my mother always thought me to be thankful to be there with family god is power without him I wouldn't be living right now (v10 Whitney Houston; I didn't know my own strength) at my mother's funeral my brothers and sisters was scared to go up and touch our dearest mother (Mary) but, I was not I went up to my mother and hug her and kiss her my tears drop all over my mother beautiful face! After the funeral I went home with my family. My sisters and brothers sat down together and we talked about what our mother told us and we had to stick together, before my mother died she said you all think your grandma and uncles treat you all like shit now wait until I'm dead and gone there gonna treat you all worsted, my mother also told us make sure you all pray and make sure your grandma give you all that money when I'm dead and gone my grandma did not give us anything my uncle tony and uncle Travis died doing too much drugs, when my mother died my brothers and sisters and I were in my grandma (Ethel) custody and all my grandma cared about was herself, the little money that my mother was getting for us, my grandma (Ethel) start getting it and she was not giving us none of the money, not one penny. It was not any food in the refrigerator at times and my uncles used to fight, argue, with us my grandma (Ethel) use to take their side; we use to tell my grandma we were hungry and we needed money to buy food but she use to reply I don't have any money one day my oldest brother Charles push my grandma on the ground because they was arguing, I ran in the room to stop Charles and I grabbed him and I told him to stop. Morris kept saying, I cannot take this no more David, look how she has been treating us and doing us m-a-n, I am tired of this our mother said when she dies we were gonna miss the hell out of her because our grandma and uncles was going to treat us nasty and like shit, and that is what my grandma and her sons been doing to us ever since our mother passed away! Author, the first thing about love is respect, obedience, power, money, and being without knowledge of the truth it will be hard to live your life David was reminded by his mother to keep hustling cause there is no one there to support you but your family. I told my brother to calm down and let us go outside and talk I told him one day we are going to get enough money and move out of here! I went back in the house and ask my grandma, why are you treating us this way? She said because your mother was not about shit, she is not have nothing I am the one who took care of you all and your mother was a ho, that night I could not believe the things my grandma said about us and our mother a couple days later my grandma took me and my brother to court and told the judge (Robert) she wanted me and my brother to get out of our mother's house. My grandma told the judge that my brother and I starting trouble and she wanted us out her house, but she was lying, she didn't tell the judge (Robert) the truth, the reason she really wanted us out was because we got tired of her treating all of us like shit, and just taking care of her grown sons and giving them money to buy crack and food, but not giving us nothing, a few weeks later she moved in to a new house, and she said to my sisters, brothers, and me that your mother did not pay for this damn house right here, this is my house now she went to court again but I was the only one with her, she sat right in front of the judge (Robert) and told the judge that I push her on the ground and was kicking her and mess her back all up she also told the judge she wanted restraining order on me to keep me away from her house and away from my sisters and brothers. I told the judge that I did not have nowhere to live, but the judge said to me, I must put the restraining order on you because that is her house I walked out the court room and cried all the way to my grandma house because my mother (Mary) said this day will come when I got to my grandma house I packed all my things I moved with my girlfriend (Cynthia). I was making the choice and was willing to change my life which I did for myself and my mother, when I moved with my girlfriend (Cynthia) she help take care of me because she felt my suffering and pain, ever since I was young my mother had me on SSI before she died I got older I made my social worker transfer everything to my name because I was having seizures, David went down there to get money because of his medical condition, it was better than going out there to steal, robbing, and get himself into trouble again remembering what his mother use to say it's easy to get in trouble but it's hard to get out it David started receiving social security and welfare he used to think about his mother when she was on welfare; he used to be very embarrassed to see his mother was on welfare. He rather be getting social security and welfare rather than to be doing things that would get him killed, it is not (v11 rich girl- he is not me now tho) worth it is not worth going to jail or prison, people that have jobs that live in the ghetto and still not getting paid enough money to take care of their family and doing what they must do that is right to survive, I feel your pain. You have to do what's right to put food on the table and to live for that day because tomorrow is never promised to any one like my mother use to say, if you won't stand up for something, you will fall for anything David used to call his grandmother's house and ask for his sisters, brothers, she use to hang up the phone right in my face, when David use to go around there to visit his family she sue to slam the door in his face and call the police on him. Author, in the book of Deuteronomy 12 it speaks of the struggles that black people in America have they need to set an atonement for their sins and give their souls to god, as Christ said eat of my flesh for your flesh is of my flesh when thou come to the altar of the lord come with fear the same as David when he went to see his grandma it was like he wanted to tell her that I have eaten of your flesh which is the spirit of Christ I gave my life to him and only him but she was to ignorant to believe in the manifestation of the flesh turning into spiritual words. Spend time with your family in the flesh never forget who had you for he created you to be like him and fashion according to his spirit. Back to the character David when he says I was living with my girlfriend Cynthia at the time a few months later I got my own apartment and I still was living in the ghetto I had my own apartment, and I was getting social security remembering how a woman was slapping her daughter and cursing her out as she turn her back walking away from her mother some cars drove by shooting at someone else and the bullet hit her instead her mother realize it's quick to lose your only child even if it's for a second she came running to her daughters aid you never know when you will lose someone special in your life. All the bad things she done to her daughter she could not turn back the hands of time to say I'm sorry or make it right it was too late for that because her daughter was already dead and gone, when her daughter was killed in remind me of my mother that little girl wasn't the only one I've seen get killed it was many people I seen get killed it reminded of my mother being killed cause I know what it means to have someone so close to your heart taken away for nothing, but I understand because my father upstairs up above says we all have to go some day (v13 Tierra Mari- stay) I went to jail a few weeks later, as my mother would say I was at the wrong place at the wrong time, standing on the corner talking to my uncle (Howard) when police officers came from everywhere, I could not run or do anything, I lived right across the street and I know I did not break any laws. You can get caught up in all kinds of things and do not have anything to do with it. Police told me and my uncle Howard to put our hands up on the car, and the other men that was standing in that area, the police found drugs in the area where we was at (v14 isyss- not letting him go) I went to jail and my uncle (Howard) went with me, we both were accused of selling drugs I made a promise to myself and god that I would not go back to prison they charge my uncle (Howard) and me with possession of cocaine. When I went to court they wanted to give me a year on

Chapter 2

Probation and I took it even though I knew I was not guilty I just wanted to get out of jail, so I was went home on bail they kept my uncle in jail because he was already on probation a few weeks later my grandma put my oldest brother (Charles) out in the streets with his son (Dennis) and his daughter (Rachel) and his fiancé (Dorothy) they came to stay in my apartment because him and his family did not have anywhere to go so I let them stay under my roof, I do have a good heart, that's why god bless me more my three sisters (Keisha, Angie, Shawn) and little brother (Morris) was still staying with my grandma my two brothers cried because they was hurting so much in side, he said the same thing I had said, our mother (Mary) said we was going to go through all this. A few months went by and I ended up in jail because I was coming from my grandma house and I went into a seizure and passed out, when I woke up my wallet was gone with all of my money, I sat on the bus stop for a while, then a car pass by and pulled up next to me it was one of my friends (Carl) I use to go to school with him he ask me what was I doing on the bus stop I told him I just had a seizure he ask me did I need a ride home I said yes, he helped me in the car because I was to dizzy to walk. So, we drove off the police stopped the car twenty minutes later and made us both get out then they found cocaine in the car, I went to jail with him. I tried to explain to the police officers that I was just getting a ride home; because I just had a seizure not too long ago they did not want to listen to me, once again I was at the wrong place at the wrong time David went to jail and violated his probation, he called his girlfriend Cynthia and ask her what was going on with her with his family she said I put your brother (Charles) out and he said why? She said because we got into a fight I told her we will talk about that later when I come home. David did not want to stress and worry himself he stayed in jail a couple of months when I went to court I lied to the judge (Murry) I told her that I was on drugs, but I was not, I was lying to get out of jail, David, received six months in a drug program instead of going to prison, David was released from jail to a drug program with seventeen months on probation he was living at the drug program David was upset because he was not a drug addict. The name of the program was called "change of times" I was in the program for six months I went home for the weekends to visit my family usually, I just use to stay in my room most of the time, when Fridays came I was ready to go home. The first weekend I went home I talk to my girlfriend Cynthia about putting my brother (Charles) out. I found out that my brother was living on some one's porch, gut I could not help because I was in the program and I was trying to find my brother (Charles) and could not. The reason why I did not put Cynthia out was because I promised my mother I wouldn't my mother felt Cynthia had been there for me when I was sick and through thick and thin, my mother also said if god took her soul away don't ever put Cynthia out in the streets my mother wanted me to keep that promise I loved Cynthia for what she did for me and I thank her very much, but it did not work out between Cynthia and I we broke up I kept my apartment but no one was staying there after I put Cynthia out because she was having all kinds of strangers inside of my apartment and I did not like that. I was thinking about when my day will would come to live outside of the ghetto destiny is what you make it, and the older you get the more wisdom and knowledge you get, but you must choose to get it and want it, this is how I made it to where I am today. When Friday came I was ready to go back on my weekend pass I left the program as I always did for the weekend, this is when I met the woman who would make a more drastic change in my life. I was sitting on the bus stop next to Amoco gas station when I turned around she was standing right there, the woman who I was looking for all my life. It's not easy to find a real woman in this world, they do not come a dime a dozen, this is to my African kings out there, if you have a good black woman keep her because it's not easy to find a good beautiful Black Nubian African American Queen in this world when I first looked at her she was on the passenger side with her friend, I was sitting on the bus stop, so I got up and walked over to her she was standing up looking back at me. I walked up to her and said hello, how are you doing today my African American Queen? And she said I'm doing fine I ask her what's your name and she said Allison, she ask me my name I told her David, the bus was coming so I asked her could I call you some times and she said I'm not looking for a man David told her it wouldn't hurt to have a friend, and she said I don't have time for a friend because I'm a very, very busy woman, then she said since you was a respectful gentlemen David you can have my number and Paige number I wish my mother was living to see this woman today I married, because she is all woman the day she gave me her phone number I called her she answered her phone, and I said, may I please speak to Allison? She said who is this, and I said you have that many men calling you? And she said I know who this is, this the crazy guy I met at the gas station the other day, and I said you should like a man that is crazy anyway, and she said why? I said because you get him to do anything for you and to you so that you can be happy, you know a woman love a man that can make her laugh and keep her happy she said to me boy you so crazy and she started laughing. She told me she just wanted to be friends, I took my time with her because that is just how a beautiful black woman want it, I did not move fast, David told her I will talk to you another time, take care of yourself Allison, and we both hung up. I was at my grandma house at the time, my weekend was up, and I went back to the drug program. Ever since that day me and Nancy talked on the phone every night we talked from 8:00pm until 3:00am almost every day, we started going out to dinner and going other places, this woman took me places I have never been before, she started bringing me things at the program I was at, one night she gave me a kiss, and David told her friends don't do things like that this woman introduce me to her family, she even took me to the business she work for. She worked with her sister, her sister and her help run the Black Business of Association I ask her how she could talk to a man like me fresh out the ghetto that gets a social security check and welfare and have bad seizures. She told me I am not with you for how much money you got, and what you can give me, I accept you just the way you are this is how I know I got me a one hundred percent she accepts me for who I am many people do not feel that way in this world today, they are all about themselves and what they can get from someone. The real people who are really in love like my wife and I please know that you cannot buy real love and happiness, you can buy lust Allison introduce me to her two sisters, Stacy, and Jill. Jill was nice and sweet to me and I love her, respect her for that Stacy did not because I was not a lawyer, or a man that drives a high price car, but I still love her and respect her because I am not like that, just because someone is nasty it does not mean you have to be that way. Her mother (Jasmine) did not like me when we first met but now her mother likes me, her father loves me and like me, if their daughter was happy they were happy. Then me and Allison moved in together my time was up in the drug program and I was going back to live in the drug program, and I was going back to live in the ghetto, but Allison told me, you are my man now where you going? I brought her a ring and put it on her finger for our one-month anniversary that we were together, I did not ask her to marry me because I was not ready for that and it was too early, when I put the ring on her finger she cried. So we did beautiful things I never done before we both moved in together and it felt like I was in heaven with her and god was praying over us, good times and bad times through thick and thin we have stuck together, this woman is the most special thing that I have ever had, this is the best beautiful thing god has bless me with when we first made love to each other it made us more in love with each other a man is supposed to ask a woman to marry him, but Allison ask to marry me I could not believe a woman ask me to marry her this is the woman who is going to have our child. I introduce her to my family, my father said ever since my son met you his whole life has really changed, he head to make his own decision because he is a man, but you have helped him a whole lot, everything about him has change I said yes because I finally have someone in my life who I know isn't gonna abuse me in no kind of way or leave me and won't tell me to forget about the pass when I'm still hurting from it. It is amazing how my wife help change me, and my family didn't why my family could not do that? That is why I am gonna be here for my daughter as well as her mother (Jasmine) which is gonna be here to. That way our daughter will not grow up any kind of way because it takes a mother and father to raise a child, and we are going to be there I wish my father could understand that I miss my mother because the mystery of death! Many people do not feel your pain, like my father said forget about the past forget about all those bad things that happen to you, it is easy to forgive but it is hard to forget. My mother use to always tell me you got so much of your father (Peter) in you, good and bad I wonder why my father do not see he made me so that I have some of his ways, like father like son one day he probably will. When my mother was living she use to talk about the good things and bad things my father uses to do, I made plenty mistakes and plenty wrong things, but I still have feelings who says that a man does not cry? The woman I'm with now she feels my pain and everything else on top of that, this woman I dearly love so much I was in prison cause I violated my probation before I went to prison I married Nancy she asked me to marry her and is said yes, I did fifteen months in prison for something I didn't do my wife wanted me to sue the officers for beating me up but I was scared to go to trial because you can have all the money you want but you still are a black man in this world you live in how many black people you know that are still being harass by white officers? I was one of those people, I was walking down the street one day with a friend and he was talking to me about how I have change my life and how he wish he could find a real woman like the one I have, we was standing up to a restaurant and a while police officer told me and my friend, we need to move from the area that we are standing in, my friend told him we haven't broken no laws, so the police officer slam my friend against the car and said to my friend, who are playing with nigger? Other officers pulled up to the restaurant my friend said this is not right, you cannot do this to me the officer start beating my friend and the other officers helped him. They beat him so bad I was telling them to stop because he was bleeding badly in his face, David was begging them to stop, but they start beating me too. Me and my friend both went to jail, that is the last time I saw my friend I called my wife immediately and she came and bond me out of jail my wife told me we are going to sue them officers for beating on you for nothing. We called our lawyer, and I went to court a month later with my wife Allison and our lawyer, the judge took me in custody because I violated my probation. The judge said we want to give you fifteen months in prison, or you can go to trial, my wife Allison sent me money and wrote me every day. My wife Allison got me another lawyer named Nick I promise her that I was gonna go all the way with it, so I kept going back and forth to court, let me tell you how nasty the system is and how the court room is corrupt the judge (Bell) and the officers are all on the same side, most of them are they got me in court without me knowing and my wife not knowing, so I called my wife before I went to court and I asked her, did you know I was supposed to go to court today? My wife said you was not supposed to go to court today, you go to court next month I said they just called me and told me to get ready for court, my wife said they just trying to get you in court without your wife and your lawyers, do not take the fifteen months baby, alright? I said ok when I went to court I just took the fifteen months prison time because I got tired of waiting and I was stressing and worrying so I said let me just take the time instead of waiting. I talk to my father (Peter) any way and he said you done six months already sitting in there, when you get ready for trial you'll be done with all of your time anyway, just take your time do what is right don't fight while you're in there so the judge can reduce your sentencing in prison but anyway I'll come back to see you (v17 Rihanna- as real as you and me) when David got back to his cell he said to himself at least I don't have to worry about what's gonna happen to me no more, the way the system works is sick. I became my own judge; I did my own investigation I did what I had to do a man got to do what a man should have done long time ago. I called my wife and told her what I did, and she cried

17

on the phone every day I talked to her I was not worried about nothing anymore because my wife Allison is a strong black woman, and she can take care of herself she worked with her sister in business and when you are into business with someone people know you, so I was not worried about anything while I was in lock up. If I would have died in prison it just it just would have been my time no matter where I am at or where I am going to be when god is ready for me it would be my last. David was shipped to all kinds of prisons because he got into fights he was not gonna let no one disrespect him, prison is a crazy place David has a real woman because his wife came to see him in prison, she wrote him letters every day. He called his wife everyday he talks to his wife all day after he came in from working out in the field his wife stuck with him through thick and thin she sent him money Allison told me when you get out of prison we still gonna sue them officers for beating you up I am suggesting that you take the stand because them officers were wrong; we all have our day when we go to see God. God gave commandments, and laws for us to abide by if we lose faith in him then how will we carry ourselves upright for he say in the morning you shall find fruits which is the seed that is planted so it can produce fresh fruits when a woman carries a child after the seeds been planted she shall conceive and bore a child for we must take measures of our life before our salvation come thither people out in the wilderness will understand the character of being a woman by keeping these laws rather it be in America or in church. David said when he goes to heaven he will ask god can he marry Allison when they both be in heaven together. When David was in prison his wife asks him could she move to Oklahoma to open a business instead of working with her sister (Stacy) David told her yes, he trusts his wife Allison, and her brother (Benson) live up there anyway, when she got up there David called her after she wrote him that is one of the things marriages is about trust! She wrote him every day and sent pictures of her beautiful face, and pictures of Oklahoma. When he was locked up in prison he saw all kinds of things happen. David, seen how white officers beat black people, you have black people go to prison for doing wrong, and you also have black people that go to prison that be innocent. Someone need to do something about that because you have black people go to prison that be innocent and have children and they die prison, well David also sees them fight in prison or each other I did not want to be around that, but I had to because I was there and in prison there is nowhere to run and there is nowhere to hide. To all black people out there that have family members that are in prison I pray for them, innocent or guilty because in prison you could die, and your family will not even know about it. Most people think that it is good for people who are locked up to stay in there because they deserve it, what about the people who are innocent and did not break the law? David was released from prison on May 9, 1999 and my wife was right there to come and get me, she looks at me and said you look nasty because when you are in prison it is nasty in there, the food they feed you is nasty, David had to buy himself some food. Now today David has brother is that is black that write me, and they are never coming home. As David said, I write these brothers it is the thought that counts, they need love because god and I is the only family they have. My wife Allison came from Oklahoma to get me from prison we spent the night at her mother's house a couple of days later I went to say goodbye to my family. Me and Allison went to the airport and got on the plane and flew to Oklahoma. That was the first time I ever been on a plane, I was scared to get on the plane, but Allison said it for me and when you marry someone that you really love you will risk your own life for them because Allison will do the same thing for me. I did it for Allison because she the one that put real love and life into my heart! When we got to Oklahoma I liked it because it was a beautiful city Allison asks me do you want to stay here. I said yeah, right now today this is where we both live we have our own house and run our own business and I am going back to school me and my wife had our bad times and good time, but we are still together today! I do not know any marriage that is perfect, hundreds of people said I would not make it today even family members, but even for the ones who did not wish me the best, I still wish them the best. Today I am happy I have my own family, and I know for sure that they will never leave me, because a real family stick together they do not break apart, I lived today to tell it all. My father doesn't know how it is to let things go, it's not easy my mother (Mary) said before she died my father left when she was pregnant you don't have to take it when you become a grown man but your still his son he owes you and I feel that way to about what my mother said, even when I was living with my father (Peter) I felt the same way, today the children that my father had out in the streets, my big brother and big sister Porshia feels the same way they are all adults I still say it's our father and I still love him. David uses to think back in the past, how can he ask god to forgive him for his sins, but he will not forgive his father he has hurt him before god makes us all different we all are not the same his wife Nancy look him in the eye all the time just to say she will never leave him there is no reason to he asks her why is she so filled with love, and so sweet? Never had any family problems and never went through pain and suffering? She said I had a mother and father that is my family which loves me and took good care of me and still do until this very day. I wish my father (Peter) could understand the same thing I have forgave him and his family but ask him to have his family done the same thing.

My godmother Susan also told me that my aunt Linda said that she was going to pay her for taking care of me, but she never did, she even says thank you, even my aunt Gloria to, and father never called my godmother (Susan) or even thank her for taking care of me I believe the only reason my father told me to let the past go was because the truth hurts! My father was buying me things and gave me things and I feel like he was just starting to make up for when he was not there for me and I did not know who he was. I wish he would understand that my father said I never brought him a tie, or never brought him a shirt, I never thought about getting him a gift, if I never thought about him, why do I call him almost every day to see how is he doing? If he didn't care he wouldn't call him at all David always told his godmother that if my father ever came back the doors will be open for him, but it won't be easy for me to forget about it; just like his father lost his wife, when he got his life together he had to earn his wife trust back when him and his wife got back together, so it's the same way for me, he has to earn his trust back. David felt like he was just starting because he did not know who he was when David was a baby, he did not ask to come in this world, he made him, so David was his responsibility, I wish his wife would understand that! Sometimes, he used to tell his wife you use to buy me most of those things I stop asking his wife for things, now I am asking my father for it, your wife is not the one that must earn her trust back, my father (peter) is the one. See I am a person that if you were to come in my house and I was wrong about something, I would say I am wrong, I will not be in my house and say I am right when I am wrong just because it is my house, that is selfish and nasty. If I am wrong then I am wrong, I feel my father his wife talks to him about me when my father relays the message to me I would be upset about what his wife said, and he takes it all out on me. I know his wife does not like me and never will. My father Peter will never think she'll be wrong just because that's his wife I have been wrong sometimes, but not all the time my father has two beautiful children at home named mark and Sonya my father's wife use to tell her daughter and son not to say anything to me Sonya use to tell me that her father wasn't my father but her father is my father she use to do that because her mother told her to and because her mother was not my mother. Vivica use to tell her son Mark the same thing, but Mark told me one day that he was not like that every time I saw mark he talked to me and said he will always have love for me, my mother always said you cannot make nobody do nothing that they do not want to do and be something that they do not want to be. When mark came with my father (Peter) to see me he always said hello and we spoke I stop talking to Sonya because she did what her mother told her to not talking to me, touch me, or being around me, my father didn't believe me when I told him these things, one day I called his house and his daughter (Sonya) answered the phone I said can I speak to dad please Nicole said he's not your father why you keep calling her? When I see them now today I still speak and say hello because I wish them the best all the time. My father (Peter) should of knew I couldn't buy him something when I was living in the ghetto hungry all the time and calling him to bring me money so I can put food in my stomach and feed my brother's and sister's to: I hope he understand that one day, family or no family when you're wrong, your wrong David's father told me plenty of times if I was wrong he wouldn't be on my side. But if I were right, he would be by my side one hundred percent I hope he feels the same way about his wife (Vivica) daughter (Sonya) and his son mark at home, they are no better than me I am still his son, I am still his family to because blood is thicker than water you made me I am still family, love me just as much as you love your family at home. I'm not home with you but I'm supposed to always be in your heart like Vivica, Sonya, and Mark it isn't no difference I hope my father knows one day, that he takes up for his Vivica and their children when they're wrong, if I had kids from a woman I will give all of them the same treatment and the same love that I have for my children at home, all of them are the same one's I made, even if I had a child that was criminal, he would get the same love, if I'm taking up for my child that is home, I'm gonna give them all the same love and I'm glad that I do have a wife that will agree with me on that some people don't and for the ones that don't they don't have real love in their hearts they just thinking about what they got, and want to give love how they want to and who they want to but I wish the people who are out there like that the best, the good and bad, god will bless me more as long as I mean it from my heart with all the love I have inside of me, and I'm living today to tell it. Thank you lord Jesus Christ for letting me live another day! My father (Peter) knows I did not ask to be brought into this world. I told him when I have been wrong, I wish his wife (Vivica) and other family members can do that. I pray one day that he tells me, David I know my wife (Vivica) can be wrong sometimes and she does not like you, this does not have anything to do with my old ways, this has something to do with that I am not her son and she does not like that at all not one bit. Mostly I blame my father (Peter) because he is a grown man and he supposed to be a man and tell her, that was my son before I married you, and he is my son now, he will always be my son. I drew a picture for my father on his birthday, he has not hung up the picture yet, he said he been busy but when his wife Vivica children ask to put a picture up, or give him a picture, he puts it up in a heartbeat. Do not supposed to get that love to. David loves his father as he explains the struggle between him and his father's wife because his momma died and now he has no one to tell him how to be careful and what measures should he take if something where to happen to him David knows life is hard but it's what you make of it I believe if he try to finish school and tries to upgrade his life money will go flying cause his mother left him with no money David should look into getting a bachelor in science or in medicine because he's a very beautiful talent I would not like for him to be like his father cannot support himself or others you should get paid for everything you do in this world trouble come were there's more money and more street game I think

Chapter 3

David could of try to get better help than to live off SSI, and welfare. Only the author can understand what I have been going through I have been calling him, he does not answer my calls so that he can let me know he just concern about how his wife Vivica feels about her kids, and what his Vivica says. I will always love him my father did worse things than I have, he has killed, he has robbed, and he has beat people he was a serious criminal, but you know what? I still love him because he will always be my father. If he was wrong or right I still show him love, why? Because it is no difference, no one is perfect, like my mother (Mary) said before she was killed everybody is not the same. She was not lying about that he just brought his son mark and daughter Sonya a car that's home with him, and his wife spent almost eleven grand on a car for him, I ask him to help buy me a car he said he would if I was his sons age, his son that's home with him is seventeen and I am twenty four and I'm still his son another reason I think he didn't give me everything is because my mother was on the streets and his so called perfect wife was not when I was sick and just got out of the hospital me and my wife Allison went to his house I was in front of his house throwing up, his wife Vivica walked out the house and went to her car and told my father to hurry up lets go. My father said she do this because of my ways I say when I am wrong, but when his wife Vivica do me wrong I do not remind her about her ways, and her nasty attitude, but my father says she do not do nothing wrong I believe he was scarred to talk. (v19 Seven Streeter- sex on the ceiling) my wife Allison gave her a hug before and she moved back like she didn't want my wife to touch her my wife just said hello and walked away and my father says his wife don't have her ways, I still love her it's a lot of people out there thinks I won't make it well to tell you the truth I'm married just like my father (Peter) I know his wife Vivica think I'm not going to make it in life, but that's what my sister Sonya told my wife Allison her mother Vivica said about me so I can say the same thing about my father Peter about what he used to be and what he use to do, he's gonna mess up as well as his wife she will leave him, but you know what I'm gonna be like him and his wife Vivica I'll wish all of them the best he supposed to be doing the same thing but I guess he's not because I'm not living in his big house that he has with his wife and two kids but I have my own house, me, god, and my wife. My godmother Susan said he's gonna mess up what he have at home then if his wife (Vivica) and him feels that way about you what he don't understand is I'm only twenty four I'm human I can make errors of my life I'm not perfect I have a long way to go my body is not getting old: I'm not in my fifty's and the way I see it my father was not young when he finally decided to get his life together, he was a grown man. I am his son and I live with my wife and I love everyday of it, there be good days and bad days, but I still love it because every day is worth a thousand years especially when it is someone who you are in love with and someone who you are spending the rest of your life with do you know my own wife treats me better than my own family does? Peter has to know that not everyone is caring like he is to his wife I see that David refers to Peter as his dad he calls him father but in the book abba, which means father which is power from above it also means god this shows that David, has more respect for his father and being without a mother can hurt but it's the heart that matters (v20 Keshia Cole-superstar) how you feel about family can be impressing to someone else that wants to learn just stay focus on your life and everything will be alright it's a killer when someone you adore cannot adore you back like for example the grandmother she could of have more mercy on her grand kids; and treat them as if they had a mother being positive is the key to a great and wonderful life (author). When he is sick I go see him my father said only reason why he came to my new house is because I ask him to come over, so now I know who is showing love and whose not, he said most of the things his wife Vivica buys for him and the fact that he doesn't have any money but he has a job and he buy his son (Mark) things and give his daughter Sonya what she wants whose at home with him. One day he reads my book I am letting him know I do not come to his house and read his books he said this is a good book who wrote it I told me I have someone I work with type it and edit my book she is an amazing author my father told me come let me talk to you I was looking for a breakthrough in life this could be it. I sat down to talk to him about my book he talks ranting about people, not having any money finally it came out can you introduce me to your friend I do have a book I want to put out and it's easy for me to do he said my wife needs more help with the kids paying for the tuition is expensive please help me some more I looked at him Peter, only god can make me happy you are a lord unto me you give me rest I think about the day and night I pulled out my wallet and gave him the card here call her she's not that expensive if you join me in my business this is how I can grow. Me and my wife been together for six years now, for the ones who thought it would be over we fooled them. I want them to keep thinking that way because the more they wish that I'm not going to be with my wife Allison the more we will be together this is where David begin to fall through the crack because Allison would be at work while he's at home alone one day David started to call Stacy his wife sister he called her on the phone just to tell her about Allison she said how is your life between you and the kids is everything ok he reply yeah things are fine I'm trying to put the kids to sleep inside of our big house and we hanging in there Stacy feeling guilty cause she's been struggling her husband is barely keeping up with the house every day he's out selling drugs and sleeping with woman out the streets, Stacy heard about her husband raping a woman because she bought crack from him but did not pay for it really what is this world coming to. Stacy ask him do you want to know how fishes swim in the sea did you want to try going to the beach under water we can go diving he said hell no I leave for the white people you lol, as she laughs and giggles she said I was not talking about those fishes I was referring to me David feeling tempted decided to put all words aside about his wife feeling trap he could not believe it his answers was ye-ah Stacy kept the conversation going ok just meet with me at midnight around the corner he says I don't want my wife to see us she made him feel comfortable over the phone she drops her sexy voice, compiling him to sin she said I'm sending a picture text look at it now her p---y was showing with lace up lingerie in pink wow David gesture was he went to room in the bathroom started to take off his clothes baby I love your p---y clearing his throat how fast can you make me come, she said bring some money and I'll show you how fast he said where around the corner should I meet with you she said 4th street on Brewer Avenue well the kids are sleeping is it in a car or your house she said my house has kids my car I'll be waiting for you there she wrapped herself in a rope underneath she's wearing a pink lace up lingerie as she waits in the car for him which is in front of her Vatican house he put the kids to sleep then David calls his wife Allison leaving a message for her saying baby I left the kids upstairs sleeping something came up and I have to go so when you get home please check on the kids for me when he was leaving Allison just arrive standing there with the key while wearing her uniform from work she says where are you going did you call me he said yes, something came up and I have to go I did not want to leave the kids at home she says what's more important than to wait for me to come home and get dress in a sexy lingerie for you I'm your wife! He says why you tripping I know but I will be back soon ok please baby do not give me that I work hard for our relationship to be strong. David deserves more but now that time come for him to explore his man hood he will go at nothing to get it for the first time Stacy ask him out he wanted to hit that feeling powered by her mesmerizing photo of her p---y he kissed Allison and said baby I'll be only a hour I have to work late because I know you're tired I took care of the kids for you give me chance ok Allison replies yeah be home by morning. As he walked around the block to be with Stacy he gets in her car parked out front of her Vatican house talking less while she pulls down his pants he's feeling arouse and he pulls down her panties as she is wrapped in a robe underneath a lingerie sheer crochet pink she says I'll let you put it in first David wanted to compare if Stacy was better than Allison and they have sex oh my god my girl Keyshia Cole was right this is the heat of passion after they were finished he says I'll come back for more she says compensate me for my night he pulled his wallet here's two hundred dollars buy your daughters something nice. David wondered about what this would do to his family he kept a secret for a long time surprisingly Stacy called him on his cell phone speaking of new things that happen between herself and boyfriend she question him about the money to pay bills but he was neglectful of his family she had no one to call but

David, he ask her what is it that he spends his money on she said David the man trying to open a liquor business but he doesn't have any money and his family needs clothes, shoes, food, sometimes I ask is he crazy tears David told her I'll be over there and we can discuss it alright maybe he's moved on with another woman Stacy speaks to him I need him to care more for his family I don't care for no other woman my girls tell everything as he was walking to her house Vanessa saw him going into Stacy's house she walked up to the door knock on it when Stacy answered the door she was shock Vanessa was standing there she said hey what up girl I saw David walking into your house she said oh yeah he just stop by as he was in the kitchen drinking wine (Moscato Rose) Stacy kept conversation for a minute he wanted to see the kids oh well Allison called me earlier she's planning a trip with the kids their going to the Cancun or the Atlantis rapid water fall so if you make up your mind just call me and we'll set up a ticket she said I won't be joining you or Allison in that David comes out the kitchen surprise to see Vanessa standing there he says oh hi what's going on I didn't know you were here Stacy said yeah she saw you walking into my house so she stop by to check on you yeah I'm fine I came to try the new wine Stacy's boyfriend bought I heard he's opening a new business but he doesn't have a liquor license Vanessa looks shock what who gave him the money! I didn't know that, Stacy looking depress that nigga can't even get a loan because he has bad credit Vanessa listen don't get beat up girl I'm sure he will find a way to pay his bills ok I'm leaving call me if you need anything as Stacy closes the door David stands there holding a bottle and two glass cups then he pours the drink baby as he kisses Stacy drink let's tastes this new drink Moscato rose vodka yeah baby then they went upstairs to have sex as she pulls down her pants and takes off shirt, David pulls down his pants and takes his clothes off, Stacy feeling the power from body do you love me he says baby let's f—k then he says I'll give you everything that pertains to this family as long as my wife don't find out about my affair Stacy doesn't remember that night she was lost in love how can I say I love a man if he walked out my life I started new life with another as she think out loud in her heart about David her boyfriend does not keep her up with love, money, and then the night came he still was not home Vanessa told Allison saw your husband walking into Stacy's house I knocked on the door but it seems like he was just checking on the kids she (Allison) called his cell phone he did not answer Allison waited until midnight for him to walk home when she saw him pull up in the car he opens the door Allison slaps him baby where were you I think you lost your mind he says baby I was at work she looks upset, surprise, work really Stacy is work baby he says I left her house to go to work I was over there cause her boyfriend wanted to fight her I went to stop him. (Keyshia Cole-wonder) there's no point of turning all of this on me you've been out all day dammit I want my husband to tell me the truth give me a reason while I make plans with me and your kids to get a ticket for our vacation shit you is a bitch how can you turn my pain into love I will always love you but you know what as she pulls out her cell phone let me call Stacy baby he grabs the cell phone out her hands baby I didn't have an affair I was just drinking please come through for me love don't hate look at me I love you. David if you were with my sister in law all day, he says I was not calm down I'm sorry for being late ok just come to bed after I shower we talk about it I didn't think we would be arguing over this your sister-n-law just ask for my help Allison believed him and she (Keyshia Cole-next time won't give my heart away) kissed him let's go upstairs and make up for sure baby I'm confident my love is strong everyone in the family loves you so don't trip if I ask my husband where he was you scared me boo. I will be smarter than any person and give you love as David talk to her about love and being honest she laughs knowing there was nothing going on between them she believed a lie and never felt that way he played her, David being fake he cheated on her someone call the sheriff because I know one day he will get caught from someone he knows or from her boyfriend and there's no one there to help him while David think out loud in his heart as for his wife that he never met an African American queen like her god took his mother away and gave him Allison as for the family that got his back his cousins Bill, Timothy, and Paul his auntie Sharon, Pastor Sheila, Sarah and his grandmother also, his grandfather Mr. Otis, which is on his mother side and his uncle Howard and brother Charles I love you all to my uncle Michael who just passed away, my aunt Whitney, my sister Angie who has much hate and anger in her heart how can you be so evil towards your brother I pray for her I can't do much about it to my other sister Keisha I keep you in my heart my brother Morris keep holding cause I think someone called the sheriff I cheated on my wife (a gunshot to his head) feeling guilty for cheating on his beautiful wife he was keeping a secret that might kill him for life people don't know anything until it's been revealed by someone else. David have changed his life a whole lot different from what he used to be, only God knows that he is trying to keep it together day by day, one day at a time, because no one is perfect. I talk to these brothers out in this world, most of them do not listen I would not want you to do something in this world and get away with it because as they say what goes around comes around. As David say I am just giving my blessing and to show that I care for these brother's and sister's that I talk to everyday my mother always told me that if I cannot make you do things right then those white will probably in jail or in prison. I feel like that most of the brothers won't listen to their mothers and some of the sisters won't listen to their mothers but when you're in jail or prison and them white officers tell you to do something you do it, most will rather listen to white officers and be hard headed, but they won't listen to their own family they won't listen to their own blood everyone know who they are out in the crazy world we live in today. For my black people that is doing the right thing and listening and going somewhere in life I wish them the best just like my mother Mary use to say you only have one mother baby do everything I say do and always respect me if I am wrong or right because I am still your mother. I wish my mother were living to see how I've change me

Chapter 4

Life, she would have been so happy, she would cry. That is why I am telling the brothers and sisters who are out there that have mothers do not let it be too late please give your mother all you can give. Someone out there does not know how it feels like to have a mother well you better find out soon, I gave love to my mother when she was here with me and then she died, and I'm still giving love to her until this day even when god take my life my spirit will still be here, author, respect those that gives you rest during the time of pain the words which I speak will release every stress and power from a man these words have no effect on any human but strength god will give you rest like a mother does her child. Well while David is having regrets about his affair he calls his friend Abraham to tell him of Stacy what she's going through and how he thinks it will fall apart the relationship between her and Reggie is getting weak and the relationship between me and Stacy is most likely getting strong I never felt strong about a woman maybe it's just sex, (smiling) but I know me and her will meet again even if it means shutting out Allison that I've known for three years our marriage will not end but if it comes to that I will man up. Abraham was telling me of a drug that slips into drinks I could make her drink it if she threats to tell Allison about our affair David replied I love her both of them I refused to hurt my lover and friend Allison had my kids we put out everything in this world for her but now I see it can damage my control of her and kids please protect my family lord I don't want to hurt Stacy for she is one of a kind with a bootylicious body damn she look like the next Kimberly Michelle her hair banging like Keyshia Cole baby why would I give that up for a date rape drug you've got to be kidding me Abraham insisted on buying the product from a friend he met at the club then he says I'll introduce you to him later I said how much a pop he looked very drastic $100.00 tell me when you have it and we'll go to the club before you go on vacation with your wife hell yeah bring it on bitch David I'm going to the bank nigga have my f--king drug ready as he took his keys walking out the door driving to the bank in his mind he's thinking a date rape drug I can fuck however I want she will never know what happen because my beautiful bitch will be unconscious at the finest hotel, damn it! I should of came up with this earlier but I never say it was me that gave it to her love don't cost a thing my god it cost a lot to me I feel like I'm in heaven [as he puts on music in his car] (v24 Avery Wilson-if I have to) David says a lot now but when it all falls out he's going to cry later remember that a dog can't go back to its vomit there's no use to feed a dog if it's dead he will regret it for cheating on his lovely wife Allison. Isn't no need to show love when she is dead and gone as supposed to be his mother looking at Allison reminds him of his mother people did not care then so why do they care now? Out of all my mother's children I was the only one that changed my life around, lived in a big, beautiful house with my wife and did the right thing. Now you can do things the easy way or do things the hard way, now I am doing things the easy way that should let people know in life what way to go, it's your choice I have learned so many things in life, I won't say I know everything, and I won't say I have a lot of life to live because I'm only twenty-four and tomorrow is never promise, I only live for today.

During the time of hunger David choice was to go to work and then after work to see his friend Abraham and tell him to gear up before he's go vacation he's planning on meeting Stacy but he does not know that his friend is recording him on his iPhone Abraham says David you only live once so lets' do things that will make you happy he says oh yeah being with Allison means everything to me but when I'm with Stacy love just got good it feels like my whole light shine Abraham keep conversation with him are you sure that you want to be with Stacy he says hell yeah (laughing) Vanessa calls Allison while she's at work for Doran B Traveling agency (cell phone rings) hey girl I got your tickets for the two of you and the kids so tell me when you planning on leaving I see you sent me an invoice so how you want me to hook that up for you she responds by saying thank you girl yeah give me for four of us and make it for night departure at 8pm on the fifth of June Vanessa is on the company phone did everything go right with you and David she says yeah he told me that Stacy's boyfriend wanted to fight her so he went to stop it they were arguing over the fact that he does not have money to open a liquor license or a store oh that's why he was drinking a Moscato Rose I didn't know ok let me print you out a hard copy then you'll pick it up I can't leave my office she was pleased but have not heard from David so she called him after talking to Vanessa he picks up his phone yes baby Allison told him that the ticket is ready Vanessa printed out the hard copy after work are you able to pick it up he said no I have something to do after work so um just pick it up from her I'm stopping by the mall to get myself a luggage to go (tone: happy) alright Hun Allison feeling deprived still does not know the scheme of David she gave a good response to him baby I'm going to rock your world tonight sweety come in my throne put all of your body on me David talks to her believe me babes my body is on top of you bye sweety I have to go back to work. Abraham calls him afterwards the receptionist came to his office to file him a work and she told David line 3 is open someone name Abraham is on the phone he said transfer to my cell phone cause I need another call out sheet and then put this on my wife's tap because she is the one dealing with that oh and a Stacy called she's on line two about can you tell her the time of meeting David said oh please don't tell my wife about anyone that calls here thank you after she left he picked up line 3 oh what up hey David it's me Abraham tell me what we doing tonight David speaks to him my wife bought the ticket and she's picking them up tonight I have to go see Stacy as well and then stop by the mall to get the luggage so we can see each other at the mall ok listen I have the PR for you so if you need it tonight you can use it on her if you want like I had told you before just put enough in the drink and she won't even know he said well I prefer natural I'll catch you later listen throw away the PR ok cause I want to be with my wife so that she will not tell your wife David sounding calm no I can manage thanks then he picks up on line two Stacy ego started talking hello, is there anyone on the phone David reply yeah what up how can I help you? She said my kids are going to week trip with their father I have to sell drugs to make ends meet do you want to come now or wait until you get off of work they have conversation for a while he kept replying that the time is not right for me but I can help you with that I'm leaving in forty minutes but can we meet somewhere else I don't want my wife to see my car parked outside your house she gave him a quick answer alright the Shalton Hotel at 45th and Dayzon street I'll be there in forty minutes ok he says bring your A game sugar cause it's just sex between me and you my wife does not have to hear about us. Abraham still astonished by David remark he arose and went to the drug store to retrieve pills that makes you drowsy he was having feelings for Stacy watching them up close he hack into the computer to figure out where David would meet Stacy then he started calling Stacy to ask her questions "hello" Stacy it's me Abraham she said so what the hell you want he talks to her I'm coming over to see you are you meeting with David she says no I'm not we don't have appointment Abraham tells her not to worry I'm coming over now I'm just two blocks away she said coming over where who the hell told you that I'm letting you in my house bitch fuck you come from, Abraham said I want to help you with the kids let me help you please don't cry I have two hundred dollars is that good she said I don't need your money he reply back oh David's money is good but my money is not enough for you Stacy alright come over David will be here in one hour he said ok baby thank you. As he was driving he pulled out a bottle of wine slipped a date rape drug in it trying to set up his friend for envy, malice, and greed knowing he cheated on his wife before he decided to stay afterwards to get on tape but did not give the wine to Stacy because he loved her instead he waited for David to come it was meant for him, as he gets out of his car wearing jeans Nike shoes, and iPhone on his left side he knocks on her door yelling Stacy it's me Abraham she opens the door now what did you say you needed cause I don't believe I'm supposed to talking to you before David come here he said yeah baby look just show me a good time as his camera phone records their conversation they went upstairs Stacy lay some rules on him look I don't let anybody come to my house you better have my two hundred dollars nigga or there's the door Abraham grinds sugar don't let life kick you in your ass speaking of ass give me some booty they started kissing she takes off her blouse, bra, and then her panties roll down to the ground he pulls down his pants, took off his polo shirt they got in bed together Stacy performing oral sex he says you're my lady underneath his tongue don't let David f--k you no more I'll kill a bitch get good with me boo. While they are having sex for an hour David call Stacy's cell phone it went to voicemail he doesn't know why she is not picking up David drove to the hotel preparing wine, flowers, and food on the table as he showers in a big tub making the bed comfortable and the sheets he tries to call her again but this time she picks up "hello" it's me David baby what up your coming or what Abraham coming out of his amazement stroking his pips while in the background David said somebody there with now baby she says it's my boyfriend I'll be over there soon. David got quiet oh do not let him know it is me ok I will wait for you. Abraham have not been rejected as he erects he place his hands on her grabbing her big breast 40DD sucking the lamb of her breast that is flowing with milk and honey making her come and feel good as the day gone by she said oh-um-oh baby I like it keep f—king me boo, and he ends it with baby my pain was turned into love she looked surprise and then smiled ok I have to take me a shower David is waiting for me as she calls out his name Abraham asked her where is he coming here she said me and him are meeting at the hotel before he goes home to his bitch Abraham does not like that he says baby let me drop you off at the place wherever he's meeting you at, she said I have my car but no thanks my two hundred dollars while he pulls out his wallet ok here you go two hundred dollars he kissed her and told her goodbye. When Stacy got in her car driving to the Shalton hotel to see David Abraham decided to follow after her just to see where she's going then he track the GPS on his car Abraham called David's cell phone to tell him that Stacy is like the hot pocket David picked up his cell phone 'hello" hey it's me Abraham listen what time you're going with Allison David replies oh I don't know right now as he records the conversation David is still driving let's see I think she said 9:00pm but I'm pulling up right now at the mall to get the luggage so what was it your looking for? Abraham nothing I think she's waiting for you at home and packing some of your clothes David says yeah I'm going home at 8pm sure alright I'll call you later peace out he hangs up but Abraham getting mad about the affair he records him getting out his car going into the hotel kissing Stacy out of the hotel he walks in behind them without letting them see him Abraham got to close but Stacy and David did not see him coming when they got inside the room David went in the bathroom while Stacy change clothes for her man Abraham using technology in the other room he checked in using a camera from inside their room he records them together after David finished showering he rolls on condom started stroking his dick getting hard Stacy helping him erect she got on top of him started stroking with her pussy they groaning, and working up a sweat while Abraham was watching in the other room through a camera he says fucking bitch you played yourself I will kill you he orders room service so that he could switch the wine for the one he had in the car it has date rape drug in it he ego was kicking in he calls Stacy to tell her that they should continue meeting up. Stacy did not answer they made love for one hour and then David said baby your good! Give it to me, shock it to me I am hot like fire she smiles and said your wife is going to be terribly upset back at home you got my money nigga he says yeah hold up here I gave you two hundred dollars so you can get the kids something thanks you for a good time. The service door man knocks on door room service he says David ask Stacy did you order room service she says no but let him in as he opens the door hi sir there's a wine for you I believe your 225 does it say that on you key he says yes, it does thank you here is a tip for you the room service say ok you can call the lobby if you need anything David was stone on drugs after closing the door he pulls out two glass cups from the cabinet and he kisses Stacy you want to drink before you leave she says no I have to be there when the kids are going with their father tonight to a weekend trip but don't wait on me boo, cause you put it down being a sexy man David took a sip of the wine and then he says wow very good and delicious I'll be on my way out after you let me take a shower Stacy says don't let your wife wait up that bitch knows her man can't keep faithful he says I don't want her to know about us boo keep it between us alright, bye baby. As she walks out the door Abraham calls her on the phone he says hey baby do you want to hang out later listen I'm gonna buy us dinner she said no right now I don't want nobody fucking calling my phone alright bye nigga, she hangs up while walking towards the lobby to her car as she gets in her car David is still drinking the wine then he passed out on the floor he forgets to go home to his wife and his kids couldn't explain what happen Abraham opens the door to his room and he drags him from the kitchen to the bathroom run the tub with water and he puts David in the tub filled with water and then he left him there. Abraham ran out the room to go see Allison but he did not tell her anything about the affair one thing he was planning to do was to show her that David is having an affair but Abraham held back his anger and he did not care for his homie David just Allison says Allison, you would of told me if you knew my husband was cheating on me right Abraham, he's a good friend I'm worried about him here's my number call me if you hear from him. Allison closes the door wondering where the hell is David as he lay in the tub filled with water back at the hotel his head is above the water that is filled up to his neck when David woke up he does not know what happen to him he came out the tub feeling dizzy and woozy he calls Stacy to ask where she was but Stacy did not answer her phone instead it went to voicemail David is speechless because he does not want his wife to know Abraham is very tempted to tell Allison but he really wanted to talk to Stacy first the morning came and he went to see Stacy knocks on her door she had someone at her house which was her boyfriend the father of her kids he answers and says can I help you, he says yeah I'm looking for Stacy I have to talk to her right now she busy with the kids is there something you looking for Abraham oh I wanted to know if she has seen David I've been looking for him as she walk downstairs with her daughter she says whose at the door her man says it's Abraham he wanted to know if you see David she said no I have not seen him Abraham insisted call me when you do. Stacy I will call you right now my kids are going on a trip with their father, so I am preparing them but when David calls me I will let you know. [as she looks suspicious Stacy does not want her man to know about their love affair] when Abraham saw Jose inside he kept his cool he didn't want to cause any problems so he got back in his car David called Abraham as he was getting his car Abraham could not tell David what was going on] David said nigga meet me at the hotel bring me some dry clothes I really don't know what happen after Stacy had left I passed out Abraham look suspicious which hotel he says David answered and said Shalton Hotel Abraham did not answer back he close his cell phone shout out fuck! While driving he saw a XL Casual store for men he pulled over and went inside the store to shop for his longtime friend that will end soon because he was in love with Stacy seeing her made him happy there was something about Stacy that he loved it was her eyes and glowing skin he told the supervisor do you have medium in this shirt and medium in these pants can you give me both please how much? The supervisor said $71.56 you will get 10% off when you buy for a hundred dollars Abraham said no thank you this is enough, can you bag it in a brown paper bag please after he was done Abraham got in his car and drives to the hotel creating a plan to see Stacy again in his head Abraham calls a couple of his other friends to see if they have a room ready in their apartment but none of them answer as he sits in his car going through traffic one of his home boys was driving his lady to work and he pump his horn hey Reggie over here Abraham rolls down his window Reggie looked at him where you going nigga Abraham said do you still have the room for rent I have a lady I want to bring by their later Reggie said yeah it's still available Abraham said Reggie you got my number why didn't you call me I dropping my lady to work now so later I check with you as Reggie drives off Abraham continues to drive going west to the Sheraton hotel to see David when he finally got there David question him about where he was why are you so late? Abraham I had to stop at the clothing store just to get you a shirt and pants ooh-nigga what happen to you why are you so wet what happen your lady let you down she gave you the boot lol, David said I drunk that wine I guess I had to much of it and I passed out ohh shit what are you going to tell Allison David said don't say shit to her I got this as he change his shirt and pants, Allison still waiting at home for her man cause he never made it home David grab his things and left feeling suspicious about the situation cause the other day he was talking to Abraham about a date rape drug but he never bought it from him so he asked a question what the hell was in that drink when got to the lobby he told the bell hopper can I talk to the manager please your room service attendant gave us wine yesterday but I drunk a few glass and passed out my head is hurting and I'm feeling dizzy wait you tell me your manager is not here so how can I complain Abraham's phone ring it's Allison he went outside to talk to her ok David is alright I spoke to him but I don't know if he's coming home because he got into a situation at the club with the manager so um I'll hit you up as soon as we finish, Allison, said thank you for being honest with me I will call him now. The attendant behind the counter could not say anything except for a card in his hand if he wanted to talk to the manager he would have to call or go on the website and complain as David phone rings he see that Allison calling him so he picks up the phone "hello" baby I'm so sorry but I got into a situation at the club I could not come home for us to go on our trip with you and the kids Allison said baby please come home so that we can go this trip I have time and patients to listen to your sad stories about how family can't get together you have a problem at the club don't take out on your family I have a surprise waiting for you the keys to the car is to be on the table and the clothes for the trip is on the front parking lot ok just come home Abraham told me that he went to the club with you I'm not happy is that worth losing your family over David be careful for life will get you down and kick you in your ass. Alright baby I'm sorry but I'll explain everything when I get home as he gets in his car own his way to her house Allison started crying cause it's not like David to cheat on her she hangs up the phone while the kids wait in the living room David still going through traffic arriving at 2pm in the afternoon as he got out the car he runs inside baby set the keys on the coffee table his wife upstairs crying on the bed David seen his daughter I love you boo, his daughter says ok mommy upstairs daddy ok David walks upstairs bad breathe smelling like alcohol he told Allison I'm sorry for everything I miss the trip you could of went without me she says if we gonna be a family why are you out in the club does our love matter shit you messing around someone else baby I drank too much I passed out in my car please understand my job is doing a promotion I went to buy a luggage for us but my boss will get mad if I don't make it out to the club with the co-workers Allison, that shit could of waited until we come back from our trip I'm feeling sad inside baby here's your bag the rest of it is in the garage she walks downstairs grab his house keys and says just leave my house don't come back here no more you cheating on me I don't like it, David you could not tell me what the fuck you was doing last night! As David pull her back upstairs, she rejects him no, no, get the fuck out Allison was angry but calm enough she did not want her kids to see them fighting David says I was not cheating the truth came out I was in the club alright please do not be mad at me I try. Allison does not care she put him out David, bye this is our last time seeing each other I will mail the papers to you or have it sent to your job David ask what papers baby she said the divorce papers you can come by and see the kids, but we do not have nothing in common no more. David was mad he called Abraham to ask him if he told his wife anything, but he is still trying to get Stacy to answer her phone Abraham did not pick up the phone when David calls, instead he call Stacy to ask her if her man is going to be home she did not answer the phone until the next morning. As David said a lot of people worry about tomorrow and the future, lots of people do not even live to see tomorrow, and as they say the future is the new beginning my mother was one of them, she always talked about tomorrow and the future, and what she wanted us to have and the life she wanted us and her to live, but she did not make it to see it, or do it with us. My mother told me not to never get married because it is a waste of time and because my father beat her to death and broke her jaw, but god made us all different I have my life to live with my wife Allison if god is willing to let it go on for a long time. You go through some things in a marriage if you really love that person for better or worse, through thick and thin, it is worth it. The woman I'm with now, not only her but we look beautiful together my brother and sister's out there should know, your life is what you make it, you have people in this world blaming other people for their wrong doing, and mistakes, they need to be blaming their selves and stop using all kinds of excuses and things that people have done to them in the pass and forgive them and forget for god has said forgive but don't forget what the person has done unto you I ask the lord for forgiveness should others that know me forgive me how can I get my wife to believe me again, when I put away childish things and become a man maybe she will come back into my life, please believe me I'm asking for sorrow no can talk to me about my love life with Allison, David, feeling homeless right now all he got to count on is his father he drove to his house to tell him of the truth he told his father that he went to a club and drank too much that he passed out in the car Allison found out and she kicked him out. Peter said what the hell were you thinking David reply my job is doing a promotion I have to be there I got carried away please let me stay here for a few days I will try to convince her that it was a mistake. Peter did not believe him cause Vanessa said she saw him going into Stacy's house David looked at him funny suspiciously and said when did you talk to Vanessa he said the other day, are you sure there's nothing going between you two David said no I'm going to get my bag in my car Allison does not understand Peter said you can sleep in the basement that's the only room available when are you paying rent he said give me one month I'll give you the rent money. As David calls Allison on his cell phone sending her a message a ring tone [v24 Whitney Houston- I will always love you] she refuses to answer the phone. People be asking for forgiveness from god, but they don't be wanting to forgive themselves, I use to be the same way, but now I say when I'm wrong admitting how it's my fault carrying the weight of my wife feeling depress about our relationship, marriage, and each other I admit my mistakes I wish my family would understand that when you're not honest things begin to fall apart like my aunt Linda, my father Peter, my aunt Gloria, my grandma Ethel, my aunt Linda's daughter Lisa and Loretta and my sister Angie. I have lied, I have cheated, I have stolen, I have started trouble and I have had lots of hate in my heart, and only a man could stand up and confess to his self about all the things he used to do, I have confessed this to the world my lord and savior, and my family but I am not ready to reveal the secret about me and Stacy if Abraham ever cross me I will

Chapter 5

Not be a friend or family to him I will always hate him for doing me wrong and unjust the first thing I learn is never to tell your left hand whatever right hand does. Before confessing of their sins they will fight and curse you out instead of telling you what they did wrong, but I just pray for them I always tell my wife Allison go outside and let it rain we both will stand in rain talking about how we should make it back to each other not having hatred towards one another I would let the rain come down on us because it's from the heaven don't you see how beautiful the sky is? When the rain has come down on us it looks beautiful that it forms a rainbow me and Allison love to see it we sit under the shelter looking at the rainbow kissing under the rainbow it is a sign of our love together I cannot stop the rain from coming down on this earth who can stand the rain? Me and Allison been in the water at the beach I remember those days when we went to the beach with the kids playing in the sand now that the time is over so what let me see what Stacy is doing tonight that way I can have some dignity I will have Vanessa drop by Allison house she will tell me if she is ok. [v25 Brandy Norwood-freedom] and while we are in the water together we just hold each other and look into each other eyes and smile, most of all we are happy together. Most people think money can buy everything, money buys lust, not real love, most people do not know the difference of being in love for real, and lusting, but me and Nancy do. Me and

Stacy just have lust for each other my money bought her, and it made the world go around it is notorious I think friendship is the key to success I have a problem with the Shalton Hotel so I will go back to ask for the manager because I really think there was something in my drink. I know if it is real love it does not have to be bought because it is for real and it is what it is, if it is lust about having sex, not sticking by that person side it is not real love, for those people out there who thinks real love can be bought that be the ones who accept you for what they can get from you, and out of you. They do not accept you for who you are, they accept you for the person they want you to be for them, that's why marriages do not last long, and relationships, and families, not just for money other reasons to. You know when I am at the house I cannot buy my wife roses; I walk in the neighborhood because I go for walks and think about my mother the beautiful black strong single mother she was. I walk by this old lady house; she has a full yard of roses growing everywhere in her yard and I ask her may I have some roses she said why? I said to take home to my wife my beautiful queen and I broke up I am trying to get back with her she started laughing and say that's so beautiful go ahead. I took a couple of them and brought them to her my wife didn't expect me to be home standing there looking at her I could not confess to her about my relationship with Stacy she will hate me for life I just said I'm sorry for not being there for our trip wow, flowers is this the way you want to keep the relationship going I said yes, please the kids miss me she said no they don't as his daughter standing there looking at us I picked her up and told her I love her my son was there I said I'm happy cause I see my kids my daughter asked me daddy why didn't you come home for our trip I said daddy had to work Allison replied nigga please what work is better than your family I hate liars I said please baby not in front of the kids let's just calm down everything is coming down on me but I tried to make

49

it right she said you have Abraham looking for you I was shock when she announce Abraham's name I said when was he here she said the day you didn't show up for our trip I went alone with the kids, looking suspiciously um David was curious about the situation cause the same time him and Stacy was at the hotel during that time having flashback of when they had sex so he kiss Allison baby tomorrow I'll be here just don't be mad sweetie give me one more chance ok bye. While he gets in his car he calls Stacy on her cell phone calling her to ask about Abraham she picks up the phone "hello" he says hey are you home I have to see you she said yeah come over I was just working out when he got in front of her house he knocks on door as Stacy walks downstairs she opens the door and says hey what's up is there something wrong he said yeah where the hell is Abraham she said he's not here David ask was he here before you came with me to the hotel she said yes he was but it wasn't all that personal David came to her and said it wasn't personal uh what the fuck Stacy I heard him in the background hell you could of told me shit, Stacy did you come to my house to argue cause I have a lot of shit to do, so what's it to you the man had something to do with why I passed out she said no, no, no, I left you there alone I did not drink because I have to be sober for my kids any way I have not told your wife anything which is my sister in law so just keep down I'll take you upstairs as she put her arms around him I'll put it on you like woo, come talk to me he went upstairs just to fuck her they had sex and then he says I will put an end to this so Abraham won't talk to my wife. It was good boo; here is your money two hundred dollars thank you Stacy says I am sorry if I see Abraham I will have him call you. Laughing, David does he walks out the house while he gets in his car Abraham is waiting outside for Stacy he see David coming out the house windows rolled up dark tints in a black car setting up his words to tell Stacy he doesn't want Stacy to be suspicious of him still David is asking what happen to him at the hotel he calls Abraham but he does not answer when Abraham pulled up at Stacy house he knocks on door that's when Vanessa rode by and saw Abraham at her house she kept going to visit Allison she was crying that her man not home no more she remember how he used to bring wait until she walks home from work and he brings her a lot of roses, he tells her he loves her and she's so beautiful even when she is home and they go places together with kids as well, to the park, visit people they see on regular everyday just to say hi then he would tell me I'm special and I meant the world to him. Vanessa said girl you are broken up how can I help you I have never seen you bent over hills before over a man she says please tell me why my man was not home to take us to the trip with our beautiful kids? While she is still crying and screaming Vanessa told her girl these flowers are beautiful yeah she says he came over and bought me flowers the kids are here they miss their father Vanessa engaging in their affair why don't you give him another chance may be he was right he got caught up with his job and they were doing a promotion don't get mad Nancy be easy, relax, ok I got us a ticket to the Cancun alright we can stay at the loft timeshare house that they have with spa, ski, and great food she says ok my kids would like to go on rides sometimes it's ok to smile and be happy. Most people don't understand like my wife Allison would say it's things like that counts and shows everything about how you feel, because it's people in this world don't even have it like that and want it so bad, most of them want it and don't know how to get it because they want this and that, as the long as they be that way it's gonna be bad for them because they don't ever think that you can do something in this world and get away with it, it will catch up with you, what goes around, comes around, for people out there who are doing it you only playing yourself cause you will hurt, especially at the end it will hit you hard. Author, do not have a lazy mindset god gave you wisdom, use it as David forego knowledge that Abraham burn him he confronts his friend, Abraham having the zeal for Stacy in his mind he is thinking I do not have to respond to you cause my women is coming home to me, he lied to David straight forward and there goes the ant, thou sluggard; consider her ways, and be wise. Which having no guide, overseer, or ruler. Provide her meat in the summer, and gather her food in the harvest, how long will they sleep o sluggard? When will they arise out of there they shall be instructed wisdom is glorious, and never fade away: yes, she is easily seen of them that love her, and found of such as seek her. She prevents them that desire her, in making herself first known unto them. Whoso seek her early shall have no great travail: for he shall find her sitting at his doors to think therefore upon her is perfection of wisdom: and who so watch for her shall quickly be without care. There's a price you have to pay for everything you do wrong, even for myself I'm not perfect I judge myself too I am a sinner, me and my ex-wife Allison make mistakes and we work it out I don't usually cheat on my wife, most brother's don't know what it means to have a good thing at home, they have a good thing until it's all gone and they supposed to be smart, if they was so smart they would know what they have at home and won't let anything get in the way of it, or lose it. David not having any regrets for in his mind he thinks that Allison will return back to him I say he's right he should try to get back in love with Allison instead of sleeping around with Stacy his friend betray him with aggression David did not know he would be betrayed by his longtime friend, but David has to stop committing adultery and be faithful to his wife as he says I'm on the black women side because most of the black women in this world today are single mothers, my mother was one of them, today most men are man enough to make a baby but they're not taking responsibility for their own child for the brother's out there that do take care of their child, and their families, and home, and there wife, more power to my black strong afro American. I love to see them go down right road, the right direction, because anything else from that is taking you down the wrong direction and you don't want that way to be you because you'll suffer and if you don't see it, god will make you see, I've been there I know and I'm telling you not just by writing with love when I write these words to people it makes a difference in each of their lives because it's what I feel coming from the heart. This comes from my soul, heart, mind, and feelings with a strong understanding! Do not ever tell a black woman that you love her, and you do not mean it, and do not even know the true meaning of it. That goes for every black women don't break no one's heart because you wouldn't want no one to do it to you I say if you can't give real love then just don't love Allison had taught me that the true meanings of the word love is to care for some people might read this book and not like it because they feel like love comes from within and it also proves that you can be faithful unlike David he was not faithful with his wife Allison it will hurt when the truth comes out Abraham started to call Allison not forgetting he taped Stacy and David together in bed holding back his ego he does not tell Allison about the affair instead he's waiting for David to make another mistake then he's going to roar like lion. The truth hurts lots of people, that is why sometimes they do not listen, they should because it helps them and their problem. They have to make that choice to want to help themselves a lot of people need to stop thinking about it and just do it, I look at my father Peter sometimes and I talk to him and sometimes I feel like he doesn't understand me, my pain, frustration, he just go by what he see and what he think my father thinks he's always right I didn't want to tell my father what happen to me at the hotel because of Stacy I wanted to protect her and her family I don't want Reggie to be mad at me for doing such things I know that my father said to put away childish things but I could not help myself when I say Stacy give me more power by making me feel good I always have to call my father to apologize or say something good, he never does that he says I do this and I do that, but at the same time he doesn't know that I hurt inside (crying) but if his son mark and daughter Sonya at home with him told him there problems he would listen and be by there side no matter what, even for his wife. I know for myself if I cannot talk to my family I can get it out in the open by writing these special strong words in my book, for the people out there going through struggle I hear you every day I am here Christ said I never depart from my people it is for them to stay strong and believe in him do not worry about tomorrow for their will be someone to pull you out of it. I use god, my wife, and myself, even people who have loved me, even this book I am writing of my pain. My father said its people out there that hurt and have problems and been through hard times that is true, but we all think different, act different, and feel different. Just because you have been through things that is bad, now today, do not think your perfect or I am gonna respond like you. Going back to the time when Abraham slipped a date rape drug in his drink have him feeling carnal all over swaddling side to side passing out for two days he didn't care all he know is Stacy is going to be his girlfriend regardless what Reggie say to her Abraham is trying to keep what he sow which is his women Stacy finally, he found a way to impress Stacy Abraham try to call her cell phone Stacy did not ignore the call she answers "hello" are you calling me for booty call Abraham says no I wanted to ask you a question about Reggie do you think he is a good man towards you and your kids she said no that nigga caught a lumber jack in his ass he forgot about us now I need money to pay the light bill they might cut it off tomorrow why did you ask me about my man? Abraham replies call him your man no more I'm here to the rescue she said let me take a shower put my kids to sleep because they had a terrific day their father took them out to parrot jungle and then Busch Gardens so yeah I'll see you in a bit he says hell yeah as long as you give me some ass baby Stacy feeling welcomed around Abraham she talks to him more than David oh, I forgot to tell you that David might call tell him you have plans but don't let him know that you're seeing me, she said ok I'll keep quiet about it. David decided to go see his wife only to make it right with her just to see if she will change her mind about the alleged cheating as he goes back to see Allison Abraham calls David hey nigga where you at? He says I'm going to see Allison there's a problem I have to fix I cannot believe she dumped me in front of our kids are you sure you did not tell her about me and Stacy he says no I never will tell her alright only if you will make it clear not to see Stacy again because then that wouldn't be right to lie to family if she ask me I have to say something about the long affair you two are having, David says, no! don't need to tell her nothing ok I want our relationship to be strong she is a beautiful black queen someone I want to spend my life with he said I refuse to hurt family I just can't do it if you please tell me that you will stop seeing Stacy now I am confident that you'll work on your relationship with Allison and that everything is ok that is all I was telling you. David came back with it she told me you were with her before she came to the hotel I can't believe what I am hearing listen you did not cross the line with me alright I just wanted you to know that it's unfair she has her man that is why I didn't pry ok don't make matters worse please I really love Allison she is my wife and she told me today as I was talking to her earlier when she look in my eyes and said baby I'm proud of you making

Chapter 6

Situations easy for me working out our salvation or our problems you did not lie to me if you did I will kill you. Abraham said I am not coming between you and Allison just promise you will not see Stacy again it kills me seeing her hurt she does not deserve this David fired back at him yeah right two weeks ago you talking about a date rape drug from a friend slipping that in her drink now if I tell Stacy that do you think she would be happy? do not cross the line brother because me and you are still friending I would hate for that to come to an end, choose wisely of what you are doing I do not have a lazy mind I am doing my part right Abraham continue conversation about Stacy from the scale of 9-10 how much do you love Stacy? Is her love stronger than Allison? Can you prove you are not in love with Stacy and that your love for Allison is growing back stronger? David I wish you would stop being Mr. wise guy and give me freedom please do not adjust the wait go ahead tell her know she will know that her man is a murder ok Abraham I was not at the hotel when you got drunk as a matter of fact I have an alibi I was at Allison's house asking her for you, but you were not home no I will not tell her this is for your own good. I bet is Allison and wondering how to turn her pain into love, David stops doing this to yourself! Just give it a rest alright David feeling delinquent I should probably hang up. David thinking out loud in his heart it is not the kids' fault that their father and mother are not there for them one hundred percent. It is their parents fault it is all my fault, while he pulls up in front of Allison house he sees Vanessa's car park out front David knocks on door Vanessa answers oh hi David where were you? You left the kids how could you get drunk at a time like this it is the summer why are you so lazy anyway? David replied I am confused are you helping Allison she said yeah I clean the chores and do the laundry since she is the only one here with the kids and I prepared meals this is your job to do but your too busy finding other things to do, David, listen she kicked me out so just back up it is still my house alright Allison comes around from the kitchen what do you want? He grabs her kiss her pulls her in for a short hug Allison replies I'm great ok did you need something the kids are going to eat right now yes he says I have to talk to you right now upstairs Vanessa is trying to see when she could move in on Allison because she's feeling loved and rejected knowing that they are family she love Allison dearly trying to go in deep with her then David walks in on her life to claim it back waiting that someday she will have evidence that he fucked Stacy, after they went into the room Allison feeling horny decided to kiss David he picks her up put her on the bed they take their clothes off and she had sex with him Allison says forget about what happen two weeks ago just fucked me baby David I love you with all my heart please take me back baby Allison replies on one condition you will not see Stacy for any reason and be honest with me about your job I called your supervisor he says there were no promotion David why would you lie to me? He says I'm sorry things did get out of hand with me and Reggie I went to the club and drank a lot I hate lying to you alright still kissing each other while his penis is in her she groans and groans feeling sexual like Romeo and Juliet penetrating her as he erects is that a yes baby your letting me back in your life, she said yes boo go ahead give me more as they finish their throbbing sexual relationship together Vanessa stands at the door listening then she started to get curious so she calls Abraham in the bathroom wanting to talk to him but he did not answer. Abraham is at Stacy's house when she open the door for him they talk had coffee and she says I want to know what happen to David cause he called very angry about the drink at the hotel I did not order room service they just brought it up from downstairs Abraham says I don't know but I spoke with Allison and he should be moving back in her home soon oh what did he tell her Stacy getting curious about David and Allison Abraham says that he went to the club with me and got drunk lol, oh Stacy says well I-I-I very shock that Allison kicked him out yeah Abraham reply um do you love David as family or a lover Stacy starts to grin what? No he's just someone I use on the side to get money to pay my bills let me tell you I don't give a fuck about him or his wife as long as he gives me my money for the booty call hey I'm happy Abraham I don't want to get curious or like Lucifer on you but I am starting to love you let me be your man he kisses Stacy you're a very beautiful women please just say yes you will go out with me Stacy could not believe it ok so what are you going to tell Reggie whenever he comes to see his kids what should we say to him. Baby let your worries go out the window if it's a problem you can move in with me alright I'll pay the bills sweetie as long as you keep that ass tight Stacy looks at him with fear, love, care, and she holds him close, kisses him her tongue down his throat he says deep throat baby he pulls down his pants she gets down performs oral sex to Abraham as he sits on couch she continues to perform an incredible act. Moving in on David thinking out loud in his mind I'm telling my father and all of the fathers that are out there instead of him showering me with gifts, he should have been showering me with his love, it also goes for his wife Vivica my father wanted me to move on and let things go but I want the same for his wife I would like for everybody to stop trying to change me I'm not like other people I still love my father and his wife with my family but lord knows all things my life starts with Allison believing that she will always be there for me through thick and thin even if I cheat on her I will still be there for her. My wife Allison tells me baby you should let your father go because he cares for you but he can't take care of you if he doesn't want to listen or understand what is going on in his child life then let it go David, after we was done having sex he created the laughter inside her sleeping under sheets, thick quilts she laughs and says ok I hope you learn your lesson look at you getting drunk when you know it's wrong alright oh lord come to my throne we are officially back to each other's arms kissing going back into the times when they had their first child and made love. David is happy his wife got over the situation about the trip now he's going to get even with Abraham as he puts back his clothes on wishing that Allison would continue being his lover he calls Abraham as he gets in the car Vanessa still helping with the kids when he left she went upstairs to talk to Allison are you taking him back in your life she looks so calm and happy yes I want David back in my life but why is it any of your worries she said let me tell you how this works ok she quickly puts on her bra, shirt and pants Vanessa keep conversation about how he may hurt you again Allison says look he's my man I missed him like crazy Vanessa closes the door come here let me show you something and if you still want to be with him then I'll except that Allison was confused what are you talking about as she kneels down by the bed pulls down her pants takes off her shirt saying you don't have to be afraid just let me show you her tongue down between her sexy thighs licking up and down as she groans ohh, um, baby yeah this feeling is new for me sugar, ohh, um, just wait until I come baby ohh, give me some more Vanessa says you like it baby Allison replies baby me and you have to keep it quiet because I still love David he was always there for me please for one hour Vanessa made her feel like she was in her throne and then Vanessa left as she left the room walking downstairs she tries to call Abraham again but he still did not answer his cell phone cause he was with Stacy. David realizes that Abraham did not do it he could not of pull that all own his own plus they have been boys since high school, and he is a particularly good person anything he needs Abraham was always there for him know he calls Stacy to see if she has seen Abraham, but she did not answer damn! He says yelling as he goes back to his father explaining how he made up with Allison and she is taking him back in their million dollar home as he speaks to him saying son you should be careful because you only have one parent which is me please don't do nothing crazy I love you and thank you for helping with the bills even if Vivica did not like you she left something for you here is some food and money to take on your journey Allison is a very nice person I'm glad yeah dad we might be moving I will call you to let you know where we going. For this reason, it takes a strong black man like me to do what I'm doing and that's being more of a man than my father, and my courage gets stronger and stronger, if my father loves me he wouldn't give up on me right now my father showed me how to have strength he never gave up on his sisters and brothers or his children I learn from the best which is my father and his wife, as David pack his bag of clothes and move towards thinking out loud in his mind no matter what the circumstances is I know my father got my back if anything happens to me he will pursuit happiness there's an emotional side to my father and that's love. Caring for Allison made me wonder how much does she care for me cause I'm ready to renew our vows so I'm going to buy a special engagement ring and then take her out a beautiful restaurant choosing life after our break up makes me want to do more things with my family, like my father said god comes first then his wife and children but don't ever forget about the child you have made and train since they were young unbelievable there is a miracle in him which is prayer oh my god! I do not think I am better than anybody only perfect thing I know is god I also know about beautiful things in life and this being a good son no matter what, the most thing I like about me and my wife is that our love is equal. I love my black people, even the ones who don't want to do right, if I don't take care of my black people then they just don't take care of each other it's those people that have schooled me and thought me how to survive living in the ghetto for a very long time has bought me to realize the hurt it can be without family or without someone to love I loved Stacy she was kind, sweet, very beautiful but I have to think about how I can grow my family to be equal and honest I know this dark secret will lead me in a dungeon but I'm willing to sacrifice my life on it lets how I can keep a secret that will tear me apart being away from Allison really breaks my heart showing I can be a good father to her makes me happy and joyful I hope Abraham keep his silence and not tell the whole world because I'm willing to keep my promise about Stacy not seeing any more makes me feel empty inside but full outside cause me and Allison are husband and wife I would like to separate our relationship because of my mistakes. I pray and have faith that the brothers and sisters that I school they would pass it along I am happy the way that I am, I am that I am, it is better than being upset, angry, stress, disappointed and worried. My father said listen to him, now it's the time for him to listen to me, I won't be mad at him or upset I'll just be stronger I know he'll probably understand when he reads this book some people will because reading is powerful and strong and you can learn a lot of things from it most of all reading is fundamental, I know because I have learned all kinds of things about relationships, marriage, divorces, and some of my brothers and sisters have done the same for this reason, I want them to read my book there is knowledge and power in my book while I try to figure out how to settle the case with my doctor in terms of what happen at the hotel. David try to call Abraham again he did not pick up then he try to call Stacy but Reggie answered her phone when he picked up her phone Reggie said hello, David respond hey is Stacy their I would like to know if she has any plans me and my wife are planning dinner and we just want her to come over Reggie said it in a ghetto tone na playa she got shit to do with my kids I just came around to bring some groceries and help around the house you know what I mean she don't have time for that shit Abraham had already left but now he has to worry about Reggie and David so he decided to do the unthinkable he invited Reggie out to a party where he can make money dealing drugs and showing his body collectively he did soon as he hangs up the cell phone with David Abraham calls him Reggie to say hey do you want to hang out with me at the Prat house me and some boys going to the club just to deal my boy has to do a show he'll try in get you in so you can make the money for your liquor license Reggie was desperate he could not believe it or let an opportunity like that go so he said where do I wait for you nigga cause I could get this right now I'm at my lady house they don't have everything Abraham speaks underneath his tongue I know she's now my lady ok well as he raise his voice a little bit ok um meet out in front of the vapor corner store I'll pick you up there alright man Reggie felt happy cause this is the breakthrough he was looking for shit he says my life been about messing around trying to make money for my liquor business yes finally my boy come through well hangs up with Abraham told Stacy baby I have something to do somebody found me a job he kisses her and took her upstairs to give her more penetration while their having sex in her room he told her I will make you happy baby just watch if things go smoothly with this job I'll be able to support our kids even more when he was finished he left out the door and walk around the corner store up the block taking a chance on Abraham before he gets inside of Abraham's car he pulled out a drink Chîroc it's a vodka and he poured a date rape drug in it this will make him feel dizzy Abraham driving around the block giving Reggie time to make it out to the corner store up the block then he puts the drink in a bag as Reggie walks up to the car in his jeans, simple shirt, and his hat he says {tone: happy} what up nigga oh shit I'm happy you called me m-a-n me and Stacy been going through some hell at the house the business came down to nothing people betrayed me and they try to steal my ideas for this business and no one wants to invest so help me what you got for me I thought your boy had a job out in a club Abraham told him the club nigga we going to take our clothes off my manager said he wants one more person so I told him of you since you're trying to get a liquor license he pulled out the liquor here this is what I have for you now when we get there you have to be on third high nigga go ahead try that shit alright as Reggie pour it down his throat he says this liquor new because it has a distinct taste yeah he says it's new you like it Reggie says hell yeah alright let's go as he was sitting in the car feeling woozy Abraham drove him far out to the lake and he says this is the club Reggie could not talk as he almost finish the bottle down to the middle of the bottle he says nigga I have to get some sleep Abraham says wake up nigga where here. As Reggie thought he was in the club Abraham drove him out to the lake near a private hotel suite with women walking around in there bathing suit music going on in the background [v28 Janet Jackson- can't B good] Reggie wishing he had a good women prancing around grabbing women hey what up yah you want to hang out with me at the club the women looking at him like he's on crack they walking away from him when Reggie saw a drop dead gorgeous women he told Abraham look over here woo Wii she is beautiful who is she call her over here Latina women with long black hair, skinny like a model, shades in her eyes, and an expensive bathing suit look like it's worth a million dollars well I had a dream that someday we would meet a beautiful women on the island of costa hey mommy you look good what's your name Abraham leaning against him saying I'm sorry but my friend had too much to drink can I get your name she said Lerna Royce, can I help you two fellas with something

Chapter 7

There are more drinks at the counter he said no we just be on our way Reggie shouting out you are going inside the club she looks weird what club? Abraham says excuse me he did had too much to drink so I am taking him inside ok nice meeting you. Reggie ask a question a bro' how come she ask me what club I thought we was at the club now I'm hearing what club Abraham it's a hotel but inside the lobby to your left is a club going on they have hot women their and good food while the music soca is playing in the background loud every one hear it Reggie decides to check in to a hotel suite so he can stay sober for the night but Abraham had another agenda it was to kill Reggie that night so he calls his friend David to come over and hang out but he did not answer instead Abraham went upstairs with him to the fourth floor as the elevator door opens Reggie is singing to himself Abraham telling him to quiet down brother I know your drunk but try not to make loud noise Reggie swipe a key to open door, and then Abraham helped him in bed wearing gloves, shades, hat, and black jeans he's in a disguise so no one will see him leave also carrying a concealed weapon as he place Reggie in the bed he took pictures of how he was drunk Abraham wait a while and then he went a got the same women that caught his eyes earlier he gave her $100.00 to give his friend the time of his life as she went up in the elevator to the fourth floor Abraham opens the door for her Reggie saw her come in drunk he is on the bed hey my friend he says come and join me I know you're feeling happy make me feel good take your clothes off give me some candy sugar I'll rain all over you sweetie she says ha you are drunk pappy ok I will do that for you Abraham wait until she takes off her bathing suit laying but naked on the bed next to Reggie as they kiss feeling on each other Abraham snap photos on his camera phone if this gets out he will pin the murder on her so he bought up the drink so that Reggie can finish the drink. Reggie says nigga you bought the drink up here and then Abraham responded go head drink up Reggie pour it down his throat Abraham told Lerna not to drink any of it because it's an investment I'm in the liquor license with my friend here and we are trying to launch our business if you want I can get you a bottle from downstairs lobby she said no need I had to many myself ok then Abraham left the room as he was leaving Reggie decides to have sex with Lerna, Abraham did it for Stacy knowing he loves her so much he is willing to do anything for Stacy his beloved soon he is planning on asking her to marry Abraham had put a large dosage amount in his drink so by the end of the night he will be dead. David calls Abraham to see how things are going and Abraham answers hey uh you going somewhere tonight David says no I just wanted to tell you that me and Nancy are back together and were working things out Abraham feeling relieved yes, I'm happy for you and Nancy yeah so you took the choice to listen to your father David says yeah you know he say a lot of things I made a choice to listen and want to learn, react to his speech, lectures everyday it's about love, family, and children that's all my father talks about it's all about making the right choice before it's too late, don't just make up your mind and say that you have done the right thing keep on doing it until god says it's time to stop or until god ready to take you away from this world, you only have one life to live, live on why you're here and why you can, keep hope alive, and knowledge, wisdom, most of all positivity. There are so many powerful reasons why I am writing this book, enough reasons to let brothers and sisters out there know that not only is my book and me for real, so it is these words I write to them that are for real. But my own father did not know his own son was an artist, that I could draw, that lets me know there is a lot of good things that my father does not know about me all my father knows is that David is still the same no matter what. Author, I get it David love his father but listen he's not a kid anymore the bible says if you leave the nest fly off the tree that carry the nest make a name of yourself when you have taken perfection into your category after you leave the nest don't worry about your home just remember when you get back your able to provide for the other ones that are in the nest. Sometimes, you must check yourself before you can judge someone about their inner being hoping for the best I wish David would have use his sense when dealing with his friends and family the opportunity comes knocking it is if you can get in this great opportunity who is better than a strong man himself is it a woman or a man, coming to his senses he sees that friends can sometimes betray you. David's father will be surprised to see how smart his son is and how talented his son is, how intelligent he can be one of his talent is writing this book, this is my college, my education, my diploma, one of my skills, and most of all my knowledge and more supporting wisdom. My aunt Linda and Gloria said to my wife Allison how could I get a beautiful woman like her; how could he get a woman who has been to college and have a good job? Allison said because I see something in him that you all do not, she gave me something you all have not given me. All they can say is we see this in David, and we know how David is, well this woman I am with now can say, she helps me change my life because she gave me a chance, you all did not she help me understand important things in life. Instead of my wife saying you did its David like my family would say she started helping me I have to experience it for myself. [V29 Janet Jackson- Rollercoaster] (you can download the music as you go along with this book experience the pain, and struggle David went through in his life, you can also get the app on iTunes or on amazon.com please share your thoughts and memories with the publishing association for this book on Facebook or Instagram.) David had a lot of enemies but I see he's trying to keep his family together now coming back to David's family Allison remembers the last time she spoke with Vanessa because she had a fun time the last time they were in bed together without David having any knowledge of this so she called Vanessa to talk to her on the cell phone, Felisha which is David's cousin came over to see the kids and Nancy but before she walk up to the door Vanessa was telling Allison I have a special lingerie for you I got it on a sweepstakes so if you want we can hang out for a while at my place Allison did not know that Vanessa can be so charming so she took the offer and said Felisha just walk in I'm opening the door for her then Vanessa says ohh, she may want to join ask her if she's free that way we can come together then Allison says if there is a price after that I will do it cause sometimes I think my husband is cheating on me then Felisha enters her home hey girl what up I have not seen you in a long time whose on the phone Allison replies Vanessa she says oh, well tell her you will call her back honey, Allison says to her girl how much you'll do it for Vanessa says girl I own my own business so yeah I can afford how about $300.00 for three days Allison desperate cause the bills have to be paid so she says yes, starting tonight and no I don't want Felisha in my business she coming over to my house to see me while she is on the phone with Vanessa Felisha put out her hands I'm getting married Allison shouts ohhhh!, oh my god! Jesus that is a big rock how many carats she said 10kt Tw cushion cut white diamond oh girl who's the lucky person she said it's a women name Berrira Kyle she's from the Bahamas, I never think she would ask me to marry her now that they pass the law in all states especially in Los Angeles, I decided to go with it because we have been friends for the past 4 years and I always had my looks on her. As Felisha starts to cry what about you girl how have things been I heard you and David broke up Allison told Vanessa I'll call you back ok bye, she hangs up the phone when is the wedding oh here is a picture of her a beautiful black women, very tall, skinny, yes she has a big butt, I love her the wedding is next summer and I enjoy our honey moon together which will be next summer too, Allison could not believe girl I have to get a dress for this wedding next summer listen the kids are upstairs playing games I have not known whether to leave them here with you cause I have to go to Vanessa's house she's made some food for the kids and I so I'm going to pick it up can you watch them for me Felisha says sure I can do that for you Allison says ok kids yelling for them to come downstairs to introduce them to cousin Felisha, when they ran the downstairs asking their mother whose this Allison tells them meet your cousin Felisha she is going to hang with you tonight I have to go get food from auntie Vanessa don't go to bed late you and your brother go to sleep on time alright kids they answer yes mommy hey I like your ring says Allison daughter she told them it's my engagement ring oh when is the wedding says Allison's son Felisha says next summer and I am inviting you to come as Allison walks out the door she gets into her car while the kids go back upstairs to play video games on the play station, so Allison went by Stacy's house to check on her she pulled up around the corner of her house and Abraham answered the door when she came out the car she ask Abraham is Stacy their? hey

Abraham have you seen David I think he was trying to call you he says no I have not got his call but I will call Stacy for you I just wanted to know if David drop by she says no he has not been here at all it's just me the kids and Stacy, Allison says Stacy alright I'm leaving in case he calls tell him to meet me home at 11pm tonight please Allison's conscious about David is very discipline cause she does not want David to see Stacy anymore nevertheless Abraham feels the same way. As she got back in her car traveling 45 minutes away from her house just to be with Vanessa, when Allison got close to her house she calls her on the cell phone saying I'm outside open the door for me or buzz me in as Vanessa buzz her in Allison walks into elevator going to the fifth floor she opens the door saying hi to Allison wait a minute since when you had all of this wow I don't believe it when did you get these things you have nice furniture's and beautiful vases I hope your saving your money cause Felisha is getting married next year I want you to look your best; be bold and beautiful at the wedding Vanessa you have to search your heart do you want a man or a women the feeling we had the other day is this going to continue, I know David is coming home now to you but really are you sure he's not cheating or have cheated on you can you find someone positive in your life come here sit down on my couch let me show you a gift when Allison open the gift it was a two hundred dollar lingerie black with sequins, sheer crochet, two piece set with the attachments, Allison, look surprise oh my sweet mother of god where did you get the money to purchase something so expensive she says put it on or do you want to see it on me Allison went into bedroom to take off her clothes and she says put it on baby while Allison lay up in her bed Vanessa gets dress and she got in bed with her they started having sex. Felisha calls David to let him know that she is babysitting the kids but he did not pick up the phone instead David went to work to try bringing in some money to pay bills and also take his wife out for dinner so Nancy is getting two for the price of one she is with Vanessa can't make a decision on if she should leave David or continue seeing Vanessa privately after they were done having sex Vanessa says next time we go on my yacht I have a boat we can float through the sea and enjoy a wonderful time here is hundred dollars be happy for me cause my man beat me and he stalk me all my life I had the worse experience with men because the one I thought was trying to help me while I finish school became my enemy overnight he was a cougar an animal I could not describe his head was shape like an leopard I was confused about how he made it in life I report it to my counsel and lawyer the judge found him guilty of all charges now that he's in prison I'm lucky to survive an abusive husband Nancy says my man never beat me but I wish you the best we continue this because I really need the money for my kids no matter how it hurts my husband me and him will be done soon cause he spends the whole day not calling me or checking on the kids I'm tired of being the only one supporting our kids. I understand what you have been going through but for David it was about his mama, father, Grandmother Ethel, I got tired of it none of them gave money for my household Vanessa says come here tomorrow that way we can enjoy some time with each other I do not want the kids to know about us yet so keep it a secret. Allison cries because she has not seen a good place or home like Vanessa's very shock to see how collective she is beautiful rug, nice couch, big kitchen, marble tiles, open floor, outside patio you can see the ocean, for the first time Allison says I felt good coming out her house on her way to the car she drives away from the facility and stop by Popeyes to buy chicken for the kids. In her heart she realizes there something waiting for me at home and those are my beautiful kids she calls Felisha I am coming home now so tell the kids mommy bought Popeyes chicken and biscuits with fries and drinks Felisha respond ok we are not going to bed, but we will wait up for you. When Allison got home in one hour she parks her car and then went in her home hey everybody is anyone home the kids ran up to her where hungry Allison says I know baby here I bought food for the three of us, Felisha, says alright I am leaving I hope everything goes well with you and David please tell him I said hi ok just let him know that next year is our wedding. Allison "I'll call you to let you know when we can go out." David started guessing I'm not doing wrong anymore I try hard to be right so I can be happy not blaming someone else for my mistakes I was serious about renewing our vows with Allison taking the advice from Abraham have made me realize how much I love my wife and family so yes, I called Allison to tell her I am working over time tonight for a special reason I'm keeping it a secret for a reason you have made me feel good and I want to return the feeling back to you I respect that you were there for my family even if my dad was annoying you stick your neck out for me. As Allison keeps it secret about Vanessa and her she says baby just come home after work I miss you the kids eat so go head sweetie I don't mind on our next planning trip with the kids be there with us he says ok baby tears in his eyes cause she is the one for him, I'm glad and thank god that I have something beautiful and see something good inside of me, and she made that choice to, if I do something wrong or mess up she doesn't say it's the bad side of me, and you stay that way until you die, my baby would say you've made a mistake and it needs to be solved just don't do it no more learn from your mistakes I have crown you royal Allison for hanging in there with me you are a princess my beautiful queen I trust you, I believe in you, and I love you. I am glad I have a woman that loves me and will not hurt my children or family remembering my mother I respect her so much even after her death I'm still praying for my mother, even if my wife makes mistakes she will admit her wrongdoing and apologize for what she did that is being honest I thank her for teaching me to do the same thing where here to help each other no matter what the problem or situation is. Just like my godmother Susan said, the ones who are guilty and know there wrong for what they did. My wife been with me for six years you do not think she knows me by now, I consider her to be wise she knows me like a book o.k. my godmother Susan also told me your family treats you this way because of trust believe in god and everything will go smooth in your life other people was wrong about our relationship between me and Allison and the kids now they are true

Chapter 8

To us and all of this is to say give away alms be courteous to one other than yourself because it was hard for me I had no money struggling in the ghettos ever since I met my wife we have been living day by day I heard in the news how people are getting killed because of money when you owe someone it is not sweet but now I am refraining from debt I choose to tell people how I have been through hell and back. This is 2015 I'm not talking about the past, I'm talking about today this is why I love my cousin Hubbard because one day we was arguing and he pushed me down and I hit the floor, my cousin came up to me and said David I was wrong for that I apologize from the heart and I forgave him he help me up off the floor and gave me a hug, my aunt Gloria, Linda, and most of my family never does that. Therefore, I try to teach the kids when you do something to apologize from the heart be a man or a woman admit your wrong doings because that is what people look at in life. But to the ones that are guilty those are the ones never admit there wrong so, I don't care for them I have Allison to thank for bringing me to her home and training to me to be a man in the wilderness I did not have the courage to admit my wrong doings about cheating on Allison I have a dark secret before it explode I will sit down and discuss this with her for she is a kind women [tears] as I work hard on renewing our vows I want this to be a special night so I got us a wedding planner she very good at anniversary's, and event planner I have never spent so much money in my life through god grace I will put a special party for her and the kids. The location for the party is by the lake it's a mansion house I have at least 20 rooms 7 guest lobbies it's big right off of Houston Texas, I spoke with my auntie Sharon and my cousin Tiffany they're event planners they know all the things about weddings, anniversaries, and so forth I called them earlier today just to say keep it a secret but I am doing a party for my wife Allison renewing my vows we've been together for six years recently I broke up with her but now I am back with my kids and beautiful wife soon to be engaged I am asking for help they said sure we can talk in a restaurant, they chose the location while I'm at work she sent me the blueprint of the design invitation cards that I wanted and how it may look at the party the monograms is crazy but my wife will love anything I put out for her just tell me how much my cousin said meet with us first so that we can discuss the floor panels and then we will quote the price for you. I am excited Sharon ask me how many people or guest will be arriving at the anniversary David said I am not sure because I have not told no one yet, um, the plans that you have sent me via email is good I need something a little bit softer not so much black and gold you know what I am telling you. Alright it seems promising so I hit you up after I leave work now he calls Allison to see how she is doing on her cell phone Allison answers "hello" David talks to her very parch hey baby you still at the house she responded yes I'm here with the kids there's nothing to eat so I'm probably will take them to Burger Foods or Will's Burger+ later how about you did you eat is everything going well at work he says yeah my job is planning on doing another show soon and I have a surprise for you so the kids can come to the event pretty soon I give it about another week she says oh what surprise I hope nothing is going on at the job David did not encourage or tell her about the anniversary he kept quiet while she talk of the kids and how school is opening soon they don't have money for clothes, it's her parents they will be coming from out of town soon so maybe her mom will buy clothes for the kids David said well speaking of your mother I would like to invite her over for dinner maybe she can come next week or before that Allison replied ok sure, I need the help but what about the ticket he says call Vanessa and ask her if she can get us a cheap ticket so that I can pay for it on my cc, credit card. Allison did not give up she fought so that her kids can be happy every day she yells oh my god! I cannot believe this is happening my parents coming over for a weekend I love David for thinking of me [tears] no one ever done that for me, which is beautiful I might make my dad choose for me another car because the one we have is too small David said do not put your hope in a car just wait until you see the surprise, lucky for me I have a woman like you because you turn my pain into love. If I invite people it would be my uncle Donnie he knows I am doing good, he always tells me he does not want me to live and act like him or my father I do not want to talk about my family bad I am just telling the truth and expressing my feelings. However, I am getting everything out and open some of this might be a joke to them, but I am serious about my wife Allison you cannot laugh at someone who has put something together from the heart warm and special thoughts and sincere wishers are with me and Allison the same, not only on our special days but I am going to give Allison my time, my soul, my love and all. I would not be ok if Allison were not here with me the power that my black beautiful woman has I adore her for that and thank god for my mother who past she created me of all things. I always shower her with roses David walks around with his wife picture everywhere he goes, her picture is worth thousand words, meanings, and feelings god created enough love for everyone, I love our father for that. A message to all black men out there treats your women right, you would not want no woman to treat you wrong. To my brother's out there that have a mother and the ones who do not if she's there or not she still your mother I always lay my woman down and rub her back I offered my wife me, and afro American king David has giving her beautiful things that mean everything to her, love, and he shares it with her until death do them apart my queen always listening to me standing in front of me smiling with her beautiful brown eyes. I praise god for giving me the most incredible woman, the most wonderful gift I have in this world it's a lot of brothers out there that don't know what they have until someone takes it from them in this manner I am teaching brothers out there about black women like my wife Allison who I gave flowers to and gifts for taking me on a journey and bringing me back safely a dark secret I have waiting to let her know but how can I bring it to her attention is it my pride or my ignorance I love watching my queen all the time it will hurt me if she leaves me again as he sits in the office thinking of how to tell his wife a dark secret Allison is keeping a secret herself she does not want David to know but soon Abraham will have told Vanessa and Allison will know about Stacy. As Vanessa went to see Abraham at his house he was shock that Vanessa drop by to see him as she knocks on the door Abraham buzz her in she enters his apartment she says "hello" is anyone here Abraham was upstairs looking down at her saying hey I'm up here holding a drink in his hand she says can we talk about Allison and David Abrahams says no I have something to do with some business plans for my recent clients is this urgent she said yes the other night he went to the club with you and got drunk I wanted to know is it true I pass by Stacy's house and saw his car I thought something had happen I heard they were arguing Reggie and Stacy about the kids, can you confirm what was going on Abraham says he was not having Reggie in the house if he could not take care of the kids or pay the bills so I guess David went to stop the fight. Is it important cause I have something to do right now she says yeah let me come up to you as she walks upstairs Vanessa notice his phone on the table Abraham quickly gives her a chair as he was working at his desk station in the office upstairs, Vanessa tries to tell him that Allison heart does not need to be broken but I want you to understand I'm trying to help my family are you sure David was not having an affair Abraham said no I don't think he was listen let me use the bathroom then we can talk about David some more maybe you are confuse or lost why would David do something to wreck his marriage. As he went to the bathroom Vanessa wait until he went to the toilet she grabs his phone to see if David have called him when she browse his phone she notice pictures of him and Stacy together she quickly sent it to her email and then set the cell phone on the table just the way it was after she search for more clues on his desk but could not find anything when Abraham came out the bathroom he says well I'm here so if you want to talk I am listening she says no I probably should leave I don't want to hurt no one but I hate to see Allison in trouble alright thank you for a good time Abraham says alright see you later Vanessa thank you for coming by and I will tell David you came looking for him she says no! Do not say anything to him just keep quiet please if you say nothing happen between David and Stacy then I will believe it bye. While Vanessa gets in her car she looks at it on her cell phone the pictures she downloaded from Abraham's phone she was very shock to see these racy photos of David having sex with Stacy so she says time to fight back cause Allison is the love of my life I will fight for her she is a beautiful women I hate to see her heart broken but it stops here the lies, cheating, low dirty love affair is gonna stop she calls Allison hey are you free this weekend she answers her cell phone "no David has a surprise for me and my mom is coming over this weekend to see me and the kids," Vanessa started getting angry I have to talk to you

Chapter 9

Maybe you'll change your mind about your sweet little husband I don't care what he has to offer I just want to see you so make an appointment with me when can we talk before you have this surprise party Allison replied ok how about tonight is this urgent you sound upset what's making you angry Vanessa I don't want to tell you over the phone, come over Allison says I'm waiting for David to come over and watch the kids sure I will love to talk to you alright 11pm I'll be there. David goes home to his wife to discuss about the surprise party and he brings food from Burger Food as he enters his house the kids run up to his legs saying daddy, daddy, you bought food were hungry Allison says baby are you home she kiss him oh great sweetie I want to go out to see Vanessa for the ticket I'm glad you came on time I'm proud of you don't worry you'll get some sugar tonight baby he kisses her and says yeah let's eat now everybody is hungry so what have you got for me she said nothing but I'm glad my parents are coming over so what was the surprise party you said the job is doing a surprise party for who? David kept quiet about the party he took her hands and kissed it he told her baby my queen I have a wild show for you here is your burger and fries with the drink like you ask ohh, she says yeah I like their whopper at Burger Food as he separates the fries and drink for the kids David still did not tell her about the dark secret or about the engagement party. He watches her as she eats and drinks the music playing in the back ground from the stereo [v30 Janet Jackson- can't B good] his cell phone rings Abraham is calling him he walks to the living room leaving the kitchen he says "hello" Abraham said hey are you at home he says yeah I went to buy food for the family while everyone is eating Abraham breaks it to him Vanessa came by asking me about you and Stacy don't worry I did not tell her anything except for when I went to the bathroom I realize my phone has been browsed David said what do you mean your phone has been tampered with tell me now well Abraham continues telling him maybe I have Stacy's number in my phone she found it that's it although Abraham lied about being at the hotel during the time David had sex with Stacy or that he even slipped a date rape drug in his alcohol Stacy will not talk Abraham David says so why are you trying to break us apart he said your secret is safe don't worry about it alright go back to your family enjoy your anniversary with Allison never give up bra David says yeah thank you. As he hangs up the phone Allison was listening so he turns around and she is standing behind him asking him about the conversation with Abraham David says nothing sweetie Abraham was confuse about Stacy and he wanted to know if I knew about it, I told him Reggie has the answer to his problem so he should ask Reggie about Stacy. Allison says oh, ok well come eat baby so your food won't be cold, David looking at Allison thinking out loud in his heart the rose I give to her from my heart I love Allison I will protect her if it means my life, I will die for her, I will take a bullet for her, most people don't know the true meaning of love and how serious and powerful a woman is, a black woman is strong, respects herself, independent, and will receive her black husband for who he is my wife Allison means everything to me I would not change it for the world. Although, Allison has a man he sometimes can be hard headed, stubborn, and ignorant, but still does

81

right by her he gave Allison more than just flowers David actually spent, $15,000 on the engagement party plus $4,500 on a new ring knowing Vanessa will ruin every plan that David has come up with she may be the one to catch the heart of Allison or Allison may forgive her man as she grabs her keys and purse she tells David honey I will be back please put the kids to the bed so that we can enjoy a night together she looked at him with those flirty eyes David says alright kids ready to take a shower and go to bed the two of you must be tired while Nancy walks out the door, she gets in her car then drives to see Vanessa when she arrives at the parking lot Allison calls her Vanessa answers her cell phone "yes" how may I help you she says it's me girl open the door alright I'll buzz you in as she enters the elevator going to the fifth floor to see Vanessa she opens her door as Allison walks in her apartment they started talking Allison says drink passes the wine glass to her Allison sits on her couch Vanessa pours herself a drink are you having any problems with David at home she respond no as a matter a fact I wanted to tell you about the tickets for my parents if you could please make two tickets to my parents Vanessa could not help it she look at her with lust in her eyes and kisses Allison your man is not cheating on you he's having an affair with Stacy one thing lead to another and they started having sex as Allison goes down on Vanessa taking off her skirt pulling down her panties putting her finger in between her sexy thighs touching the lips with her finger going in and out licking up and down with her tongue while Allison is asking her to please give me the ticket and some money baby I'll give you anything you need Vanessa feeling horny ohh, uh, um yes, baby oh I'm feeling rush today keep it coming baby for one hour this is incredible give me more baby as Allison work her way up Vanessa's breast sucking it with purity holding it with both hands squeezing her breast touching the nipple as she continues to suck Vanessa have orgasms taking turns now you do me honey as Allison sits on the couch letting Vanessa do the same to her. David feeling lonely decides to call Abraham back but he did not answer his cell phone, so he calls Stacy but she was with another man named Willie as she remembers Abraham telling her if she ever needed something to call him but Willie wanted to meet with Stacy he sells drugs and owns a clothing store not too far from David's job Stacy is glad that he came over to fuck and give her money yes she did whatever it took to provide for her kids since she has not heard from Reggie for one week as Abraham drives over to Stacy's house he notice a car park out front so he gets out the car and knocks on door she did not answer the door Stacy was too busy f—king Willie upstairs so he tries to call her one more time and Stacy finally answers her phone he says hey I'm outside she tells Abraham can you come back later I am busy right now he hears a man voice in the background oh whose that I hear someone is that a man Stacy says no it's my brother he came over to bring me food for the kids Abraham replies oh I was coming over to pick up the kids and you to go get something to eat Stacy says come back later she hangs up the phone and continues having sex with Willie. As Jill which is Allison sister decides to pop in to check on her older sister when she came at the door of Allison house Jill had her cell phone in her ears listening to music as she repeats the words Jill says hey girl where have you been? You did not call me or nothing let me in Allison says ok I have not seen you in a while Jill answered yeah I need some money or food for my kids it's been what like three weeks since I last saw you, you were talking about moving in with David she said yeah we broke up recently and I took him back in he had to go live with his father I'm sorry but cash is low in my family I have food though come in the kitchen while the kids are playing video games upstairs did you hear that Stacy found a new man Allison said who is this new man she said Willie he came over my house to get some uh, and I hit it he gave me two hundred dollars girl so I can pay my rent people don't understand how hard it is to raise kids in this life so he left your apartment to sleep with Stacy is this prostitution hell no Jill shouts what do you think I am a slut I gave him my ass because he's cute my hormones was flying off the shelves when he came to my house I couldn't help but notice his biceps and triceps he had ripples ohhh, a black brother with a PHD, pretty hot and dark he's a handsome brother I love me some him I never felt that way before ohh, go head Toni Braxton you are a Chamillionare please don't talk about Willie in my house when you know I am with David Jill could not help but to be curious so how is David treating you? Is he always there for you now that your back together Allison replies yes he is, and I know that there is nothing between us well the reason why I came here is because I live on the second floor of Vanessa's apartment me and her had dealings with each other the same thing she did to you happened to me you went to visit her what happen did you two talk? Allison could not tell Jill so she won't tell David she loves him so much she's willing to save her marriage at any cost in her mind she kept quiet about it now we had a drink I talk to her about tickets for my parents to come over um, there visiting next week Jill look surprise oh my gosh you mean our parents are coming over as she look at Allison with understanding knowing that something may have happen Jill requested that Vanessa continues to help the family so when are they coming girl give me the scoop Allison says as soon as David can tell me when the surprise party will be at his job they doing a promotion and David invited all of us to come. Jill girl I thought she went down on you Allison why you look so far away did something happen tell me Allison says no, nothing happen between me and Vanessa it's strictly business Jill says ok just business yeah says Allison just business well give me the food and let me go I have tones of chores to do at the house and my daughter may be here later to meet the other kids as she was leaving Jill was wearing Spanx, tennis shoes, tank top, shades, gold loop earrings, and her hair was black, blue highlights with some blonde mixed in her hair. David coming home to find Allison sleeping in the couch as he looks at her pulling hair back while the kids are upstairs saying in his mind she knows the respect and strength her black man has because it takes a strong, strong, black man and a hardworking man to handle a beautiful black women like Allison she's very gorgeous I stand up for my queen, I'm proud to be the man of the house, at times I may sit my wife down in the chair washing her hair over the sink and then drying her hair, putting grease in the scalp all throughout her hair combing it through so she can style it later I don't think Allison remembers me taking care of her like I do my daughter most people would think that it's narrow to be the man who takes care of their wives but I am he that was there for her no matter what the cost is. I have talk to men about their wives and showing them how to be with their wives sometimes it goes in one ear and out the other giving the teaching of how to take care of the sisters just like you would if she was your mother, most of them don't even be on that level for the brothers that do take care of their women congratulations on your hard work be kind to one another, pray for each other, come together as one don't make things difficult in your life I made a prayer to the lord saying I shall never leave her spiritually or physically if I was to ever leave this world then my wife can have the lonesome of cash coming out of me when you pierce the flesh which is my body you'll see money instead of blood I wouldn't want her to suffer I like did growing up. It's for my kids and my beautiful wife so she can say I had a good husband, as David went upstairs he peeped his head in the children's room to see what they're doing as his daughter ask him daddy when can we see our grandparents momma said next week and his son says are they coming father David said remember I told you I have a surprise for mommy Allison woke up she heard someone upstairs sounding like David she walked upstairs to see David she overheard the conversation about the surprise while David in the room with the kids he pulls out a ring box showing the kids this expensive ring and he says I'm renewing my vows with your mother of course for our anniversary when Allison heard this she cry because she kept a dark secret about Vanessa but Allison went to the other room crying in the bathroom of the master bedroom then David could not help but to check on Allison he went in her room saying honey what's wrong she said nothing baby I just woke up and believe though me things just happened I guess so what do you want to eat he said I saw Jill pulling out oh she came by to get some money I had twenty dollars so I lend it to her David didn't mind he says let's go out to eat I want pizza hut honey do you have any money she said yeah the kids are excited they scream ya were going to pizza hut can we bring our bear David reply yeah sure get

Chapter 10

Your coats and put on some shoes were leaving right now Allison stayed behind honey wait for me I will be ten minutes I have to use the bathroom he says alright as he walks downstairs to the car with the kids. Allison waits until he gets in the car she calls Vanessa hey girl I left you a message already please give me a call because I am gonna take you up on your offer while Vanessa is watching David have sex with Stacy on her cell phone Vanessa did not answer her phone she was so upset crying because this may be the women she chose to be with which is Allison. As Jill calls her to see how she is doing because Vanessa did not go to work that day, Vanessa still did not answer her phone. Allison walks downstairs to the car after that they left driving to pizza hut Allison feeling repelled she says what were you and the kids talking about David cut in the conversation honey you can invite your parents over Monday, she looked at David Monday that's in two days he says yeah I will pay the ticket baby oh my god says Allison the party will be on Tuesday the kids can come over there will be food, drinks, music, and chairs, table for us to eat we have a long list of people so um, yeah baby be happy for us because I have a special surprise for you ok honey. The kids are jumping up and down saying yes, the first time momma and daddy are together we go out yeah David saying this is family we shall never be separate alright I'm glad to be on the same level as the brother's out there how they take care of their women just like my father care for Vivica they know to do the right thing it's everlasting power to be there for your family I'm not ghetto anymore ever since Nancy took me in to be with her all of my problems went out the door this is how my pain turn to love, keeping the weight down between me and Stacy so Vanessa calls Allison while she's in the car she could not hold back her tears Allison answers "hey girl" very happy to hear from Vanessa you can make the ticket for Monday early the departure time will be 10am and the arrival time will be 1pm me and David will pick them up at the airport thank you for calling what's wrong you sound disturbed, Vanessa says girl meet me tonight at my house o.k. because I think you should hear it from me I'll have your ticket ready for Monday but try to come over I'll be waiting for you. Allison says well ok sure I drop by tonight Jill came over she said that two weeks ago she saw me going into your apartment that she lives on the second floor I told her we had drinks and talk about the surprise party, but I will tell you the rest when I go over your house, alright do not sound down try to find something that will cheer you up. David going astray daydreaming while driving thinking out loud again in his mind saying I am gonna always keep my African queen happy by giving her whatever she needs whatever I feel like that is happy for her and for me to keep us together. See I keep her happy by giving her love and affection being sexual with her my dick can do all things with power I am blameless of it because she is my power it's her that rejuvenate my heart the laws of nature is sex in my book after tonight I'mma make her happy by taking her under the sheets f—king her day and night let her feel my shaft until it get to the top she can stroke it all she want cause I trust her my beloved wife piercing me with her sexy body, long hair, beautiful looks, I can't control my hormones around her as David completes his thoughts about Allison he pulls up inside of pizza hut while parking he says baby I have to go to the rest room go head and order the food find a table I'll be right back when he went in the bathroom he pulls down his pants pull out his penis as he stroke back and forth in the stall David could not hold back his orgasms he erects the noise of someone thrusting his dick David, arouse no more it went down he washes his hands then went to meet his family telling his wife when I look at you I bust kissing his wife inside the restaurant telling her I love you baby, she said let's eat and then we'll go home and finish talking before I meet with Vanessa tonight David says I can't give you everything but I would die trying the day I said I do to Allison that day came and filled my Afro-American queen heart she was ready and so was I we both knew the answer before we ask each other because we really truly in love, were just not only in love with each other but we are also about staying together until death do us part, even we wish each other the best every day and many more. David eating pizza with beef, pineapple, veggies, and mushrooms as he orders for his wife and kids two large boxes of pizza it is not about what other people think but to all my homies praying for us and want us to stay together I give them the same love back. I love the people who are married that respect their spouse and doing something about it they are going somewhere in life and always doing it positive not ignorantly. I am proud of my black people who is working harder to get better and better. The woman I hold in my arms everyday close to me, Allison can lay her head on my shoulder, we both are emotional and most of the time it takes time for us to let each other go. When they were finish at the restaurant Allison says honey what happen in the bathroom are you okay he says baby yeah I'll explain it at home not in front of the kids as they got in there car Allison did not mention the love affair with Vanessa because she needed the money to take care of her family and David would be very upset while Vanessa sits home kindle the fire rehearsing what she should say to Allison how she is going to react to this horrific affair between him and Stacy. David drops the kids off went upstairs with Allison put the kids to sleep then they went in their room to have sex David says to Nancy baby this is what I was trying to say as he demonstrates the dick arousing in front of her he grabs her hand stroke it for me please darling, my dick is up I could not hold it down she immediately performs oral sex on David making him Allison feel like a man ohh, uh, David is laying on her bed baby give it to me she takes off her clothes and then they had sex. Vanessa fell asleep she could not keep her eyes open anymore instead she went upstairs to her bed showered before she went to sleep crying in the shower feeling lonely then she decides to call Jill but she did not answer, so Vanessa went to sleep early that morning Allison calls Vanessa hey girl I will be coming by cause David is spending time with the kids I'm sorry I could not come me and him had a wonderful time together especially in the bed as she laugh out loud Allison was in the car when she called Vanessa, well I have to do some shopping for the surprise party and then I am coming to your place for the tickets okay love bye. Vanessa heard the message and she just could not answer the phone Vanessa went out to the gym, she saw the instructor for the yoga class Vanessa is doing yoga her phone rings an hour later she answers hello, how can I help you? It is me Allison you did not pick up your phone is everything okay she said yeah pretty much you stood me up last night Allison says look home girl I have a man that treats me right honey he gave me some sugar last night dammit! What about you are you okay I am sorry Vanessa, please do not be mad just get your butt over here alright bye. Allison says I can't believe that bitch hung up on me well as she drove to Vanessa house walking up to the elevator Jill was walking out the lobby she see Allison hey girl Allison it's me Jill she says oh where you was going, Jill says what in the world are you doing here she says I'm here to pick up the tickets from Vanessa ohh girl you going upstairs to see Vanessa I know all about that baby you're not fooling me go head go down there boo as Jill reach her hands over to Allison between her thighs showing her what to do with Vanessa then she walks away Nancy just stood there looking at Jill are you crazy I would never do that bye. Allison was curious as to what Vanessa was crying about so she went up the fifth floor and spoke with Vanessa knocks on door Vanessa opens the door hey Vanessa looking like hell her hair all over the place you just coming from the gym says Allison, Vanessa, says close the door come here let me talk to you there is something I want to show you as Allison pour herself a drink Vanessa grabs her cell phone scrolling down on her iPhone playing back the video between David and Stacy when Allison saw the whole thing she screams ahh! ahh! David bought me a ring for our anniversary I heard him telling the kids yesterday he's gonna surprise me at the party, [crying] where the hell you got this video from she said Abraham I went over to his house to ask about Stacy constantly men are leaving her house in and out, oh my god you did not know sugar I still love my man but damn I'll be damned if he cheats on me baby he did it more than one time you took him back Allison says I spent all day with him yesterday after work he came straight home. As Allison cries on the couch Vanessa pulls her in the room come over here boo, he has a dirty dark secret so do you because you have been coming over having sex with me I believe the both of you have to clear your chest alright so Allison feels neglected she says fuck it let's do it I still in love with him but I need the money Vanessa says don't renew your vows until you know that your man is not cheating on you and your not cheating on him but you see all of that is going to change because if I am giving you money then you have to be my lady how about it boo make up your mind Allison gave up she was desperate for money yeah I'm in let me uh, could not believe what she saw Allison turns around give me your phone download this on my phone I'm coming baby okay just let me download the video to my phone and save it. As Vanessa calls Allison to come to the room baby she enters in takes off her clothes and perform sexual activity on her pulling her panties down wearing nothing but a dildo piercing her vagina in and out making Vanessa feel welcome as she has orgasms, Allison felt the same way so now she knows about the affair Allison will get even when she gets home. As David calls Sharon and Jill over the phone Sharon says yeah everything is in place the only thing is your guest will be arriving a little late because the car they rented broke down on the highway so other than that it's complete David reply alright just send me pictures of the place and how it looks or send it to my emails okay Jill says yeah I saw your wife going to Vanessa's apartment to get the tickets for her parents alright they will be coming in on Monday so were ready for your surprise party engagement David feels reluctant and says finally my wife will have the time of her life yeah tonight is when I will ask her to come to the hotel near the event thank you so much. When Allison got home she threw her keys down headed upstairs to David directly he says hey did you get the tickets she said baby when I ask you about Stacy the other day you said she was having a fight with her boyfriend and you went to stop it, David didn't answer honey what's happening oh I spoke with Sharon and she says the place is ready so we can move in to a hotel near the event Allison slaps him crying, screaming, what the hell did you do to her David does not know if Abraham told her or what but he tries to keep her calm look at this baby she took her cell phone play the video back of him having sex with Stacy at the hotel standing in front of him waiting for a confirmation, sweetie this is private where did you get this Allison says Abraham had it in his cell phone David getting mad turning black and blue looking at Allison, I did not want to hurt you I got drunk and we made love it was one time my god he grab his keys where are you going David Allison says he was speechless, heading to Abraham's house with his gun in his bag David did say if anybody come between me and his wife he will have to kill them I don't care who it is. Still David did not answer Allison he just went in his car drove off to Abraham's house when Abraham least expected him to come over angry David knocks on door Abraham open the door letting him in David took a good look at him saying you lied to me bra, my wife found out about me and Stacy you son of a bitch pushing Abraham to the floor. Abraham got up and said I never spoke with her she never came to my house David smiling you told me that you were not at the hotel that day when me and Stacy was fucking so how did my wife get the video off your phone of me and Stacy fucking Abraham says you mean after you got drunk listen I lied for you I don't know the only person that came here asking for you was Vanessa David I'm no fool as Abraham walks slowly backwards David don't do anything stupid because I honestly don't know how she found out. David said she went to see Vanessa nigga she downloads the video off your phone your stupid bitch you recorded us using it as leverage I thought we was boys your supposed to have my back not burn me damn it! Abraham could not understand so he says let me call Vanessa and ask her why she did this horrific crime as he reach in his drawer Abraham pulls out his nine millimeter gun shots at David but reluctantly David shot back at him hitting Abraham in the chest David got shot on the chest as well the neighbor heard the argument and calls police they both did not make it as the doctor at the hospital calls Allison to tell her that David has pass away from a bullet wound and so has Abraham police officers went to the house to question Allison and all she could say was my man had an affair I confronted him about it and he went off to his friend's house but I did not know he had a gun. While she was being questioned [crying] Allison calls Vanessa to tell her help me David died so did Abraham, they shot each other than Vanessa calls Sharon and Jill to say that the party is over keep the money because David died from a gunshot wound apparently Abraham took a shot at him and David returned fire they both died at the hospital Allison is going there now to see her husband she is now a widow. Sharon calls Nancy but she did not answer so she drives to the hospital meets up with Allison and says to her don't worry about a thing I'm glad it's over girl he wanted to make it up to you so he got you this as Sharon shows her the blueprint of the anniversary party that David left for her Jill came over in a rush with her kids running to Allison baby cry on my shoulders sweetie I'm sorry to hear what happen soon you'll get over it. David was a good man sugar okay just forgive and forget don't let it get to you be pretty move on I'm sure there's someone else for you the next morning Allison went to the event just to tell the family that David was a good man he planned an anniversary for me and the kids to be invited I wanted nothing more but to see him alive even if he had cheated on me I forgave him because that was my man I had his back through thick and thin. Thank you all of you are my beloved the kids walk up the front to hug their mother as she cries Allison made the announcement that the funeral will be held at St. Baptist church on Elway street please show up god bless you all. People ate at the anniversary party and they laugh at the good times that David and Abraham was good friends through high school and college knowing that Allison will never be with another man she talks to Vanessa on the side in the bathroom with no one else but them, Vanessa hugs her and says baby the truth has to come out baby whenever you are done mourning your husband David give me a call okay she pulls her back and says kiss me just do it Vanessa could not believe the reaction that Allison was giving her, so they kiss and she says come over tonight I'll make love to you I still need help paying for his funeral and paying the bills, never the less packing my late husband things please make me feel good tonight after I put the kids to sleep I want you here with me Vanessa took her in to her life ever since then Allison learn her lesson don't ever cheat on your soul mate as she pray for his family, father who was speechless at the funeral about his son David he talk for a while and then broke down and cried peter just could not hold his peace he looked at Allison in the funeral and told her you were the best thing that ever happen to my son David he praise you always believe it, I love you for taking care of my son your still my beloved daughter in law thank you. Allison just went home to be with Vanessa because she is the first women she has ever been with and the last. To be continued.

Printed in the United States
by Baker & Taylor Publisher Services